PREMONITIONS
BOOK 2: WAR

Creative Texts Publishers products are available at special discounts for bulk purchase for sale promotions, premiums, fund-raising, and educational needs. For details, write Creative Texts Publishers, PO Box 50, Barto, PA 19504, or visit www.creativetexts.com

PREMONITIONS: BOOK 2: WAR
by Diana E. Anderson
Published by Creative Texts Publishers
PO Box 50
Barto, PA 1950
www.creativetexts.com

Library of Congress Control Number: 2018953092

ISBN: 978-0-692-16410-5

Dedication

This book is dedicated to all of the military personnel who have served this great country of ours, past, present and future, and to their families who also served.

"Freedom is not free."

PREMONITIONS
BOOK 2: WAR

DIANA E. ANDERSON

Creative Texts Publishers, LLC

Barto, PA

Acknowledgments

There is no way I could have written Book Two without the help and encouragement I received from my friends and family. My husband, Michael, as usual, has been my rock. I am so grateful for his patience while I sat at the computer every night for hours writing away. I'd like to also thank my friends Jennette Larsen and Renee Davis, who were constant sources of support and encouragement.

CHAPTER ONE

I have been experiencing vague premonitions on and off for the last few months, which was both good and bad. It was good in that it helped my family, my friends, and me prepare for the economic collapse of the United States. It was bad because every time I started feeling that sense of foreboding, I knew something else was about to happen.

This afternoon, I had a terrible headache and laid down for a bit to try to ease the pain. I had a terrible nightmare and woke up screaming. In my dream, the Homeland forces decided to set off an EMP against the rest of the country as part of their plan to institute a New World Order and a new form of government in the United States – one not guided by our Constitution. When I awoke, I *knew* this EMP was coming, and Tom and I rallied everyone to make sure everything that could be ruined by an EMP was either disconnected or put somewhere safe. I felt really foolish as we were racing to get it all done, but I'd rather feel foolish than lose even one little bit of the civilization we had been fighting to hold onto.

We had a quick and simple dinner, and then got all the kids and most of the adults settled in the basement with lots of blankets and pillows and a big pile of board games. Tom and I were trying to play along, but I began to feel that old familiar foreboding in the back of my head. It was getting so strong, I could feel my hands starting to tremble. I told Tom I needed to go outside for a few minutes to get a breath of air. We stepped out onto the front porch, and found Carter coming up the front steps. He looked like he had just ran a marathon, out of breath and sweating. He told us he came to let us know he just heard from headquarters at Fort Bragg that they were evacuating the base as quickly as they could because of planes inbound from the east over the ocean, presumed to be Homeland planes.

"We have a lot of equipment there, but not enough to fight what is coming, and so they are trying to salvage what they can in case these inbound planes plan to strafe or bomb our equipment. I wanted to let you know, just in case you see planes landing near here. They may be ours."

I felt a chill, and Tom put his arm around me. "Carter, you don't think these inbound planes are going to set off an EMP, do you?" I could tell by his stricken face that he thought that was exactly what was going to happen. "How many people are still at Bragg?" I asked.

"I honestly don't know. I know that they've been moving people and equipment around for a while. They started evacuating military families about a week or two ago. I know they were putting as many troops on planes and helicopters as they could to get them away, and a lot of troops left last night in MRAPs, trucks towing tanks and missile systems, and all other kinds of military vehicles. There was talk in the upper echelons that Homeland might try to invade Bragg, which is another reason why my guys and I are here."

Carter began to pace back and forth in front of the porch. Tom and I stepped down to just walk with him and try to help him calm down and stop pacing. Although I had not known him very long, Carter did not seem to be the kind of person who fell apart easily. Suddenly, he stopped walking and looked at us. "Denise, Tom, I am so sorry. I didn't mean to lose it in front of you. I've had the same feeling as you have for about the last two weeks. I reported it up the chain of command, and they listened to me, but I wasn't sure they were taking it seriously until just now when I got word about the evacuations. At least the majority of folks must have escaped from Bragg, and any left are hopefully in bomb shelters before the Homeland planes arrive. I suspect Homeland plans to bomb the daylights out of Bragg and make it useless for us."

"Do we need to worry about them coming this way?" Tom asked, and Carter shook his head no.

"I don't think we are worth it for all of the extra gas they would need to fly this far. AV fuel is pretty hard to find these days." By now, Carter was much calmer, and we were standing in the middle of the front yard.

"I didn't tell you about Bragg to begin with because I didn't want to worry you any more than you already are. I know you already have so much on your mind, and battling Homeland is my job, not yours."

"Hey now, Tom and I both took an oath to 'support and defend the Constitution of the United States against all enemies, foreign and domestic'. That oath didn't stop just because we no longer wear a uniform. We're in a war for our way of life and all of us need to be involved, not just the current active duty troops. Let's go back to the house so you can tell us what else you have not already told us, and so we can figure out how we can support you with more than meals and watching over the dependents."

Carter opened his mouth to say something when suddenly, the entire sky to the southwest lit up in a brilliant white light. Carter looked at the light for a second, then said, almost to himself, "I'll be damned, they did it." He looked at Tom and I just standing there, horrified at the light, and said one word: "RUN!"

Tom grabbed my hand, and the three of us took off for the front porch. As we ran into the house, Tom was yelling for everyone to take cover in the basement and to shut all the doors. Naturally, that got everyone in the basement area upset, and some of the younger kids began to cry. We made it to the bottom of the basement stairs and while Tom secured the door, I started a head count. "Is anyone missing?" I asked. Carter was on the other side of the basement door trying to reach his troops, but it seemed like there should have been more people.

Bill responded, "Mark, Red, Frank, and Scooter are over at the berm with some of the Marines pulling guard duty right now, but everyone else is here. What happened?" I tried to answer, but my mouth was so dry and I was shaking so badly, I couldn't get the words out. Tom answered for me.

"It looks like Fort Bragg was just nuked."

There was a sudden deathly silence in the room; even the crying children got silent. "We don't know that for sure, but there was a brilliant flash of light that way, and Carter told us that there were Homeland planes headed towards Bragg. We don't know if it was a ground strike, or even if it really was a nuke, and we don't know if it was an EMP." I looked around at all the people in the room who were so dear to me. Their faces were shadowed in the low light of the emergency lanterns and reflected the fear we all felt.

"What about radiation? What's going to happen?" asked Stacy. "Are we safe here?"

"I don't really know. We saw the flash, but we didn't feel any explosion or vibration, at least I didn't. Did anyone?" I looked around and people were shaking their heads no. "We didn't hear anything, either. There was not any air blast that we know of, so I would venture to say that if it was, in fact, a nuke, it was a very small one. Hopefully, the wind will continue out of the west, and if there is fallout, it will blow away from us rather than towards us. Until we figure out the radiation thing, though, we need to keep everyone down here for now." I jumped up quickly. "I just remembered I have several Nuk-Alert key fobs hanging on a hook in my office upstairs. That would at least tell us if we were being exposed to radiation. I'm going to run upstairs and grab them."

Tom stood up and blocked the basement door. "It is too dangerous for you to go up there right now. Wait until we have more information and we know if it is safe or not."

I shook my head adamantly. "I don't think there is any real risk. Even if that was a major nuclear detonation, it takes time for radiation to reach us. And, the wind is blowing it away from us, not towards us. I think it is worth the risk to just run up there and grab the fobs."

Tom started to argue with me.

"No arguments. I promise I'll just grab the fobs and come straight back." I stood resolutely in front of Tom. Eventually, he shrugged his shoulders and stepped away from the door.

"I promise I'll be right back." I climbed the stairs, shutting the basement door behind me. Carter was nowhere to be seen. When I got to the door at the top of the stairs, I had a minute or so of panic, worrying what I would see on the other side of the door. I took a deep breath, opened the door, and... nothing. It was peaceful and quiet. I looked out the window, but I couldn't see anything out of place. I ran into the office and grabbed the four fobs hanging there. Silence. The little alarms were not making any noise. I knew the fobs were working because I had taken them to the hospital when I first got them about a month before this entire mess started. I brought them to the radiology department and put them on a tray in a room where they were getting ready to do an x-ray. As soon as the x-ray machine turned on, the Nuk-Alerts began to chirp. The radiologist said he had one too, and that they were always on and lasted about ten years. He kept his in his office so it didn't chirp all day, and he assured me that it would chirp long before there was enough radiation to cause any harm.

I found Carter on the front porch and handed him one of the Nuk-Alerts. By now, he had caught his breath, and was busy trying to get hold of some of his men on the radio. He had a brief conversation, and then turned to me. "I doubt the radiation would have time to reach us, especially since the wind is coming out of the west and blowing any fallout away from us. I think you are safe for now to let folks go upstairs as long as we have the alarms, but we'll need to be ready to head back downstairs if the alarms start sounding. I would suggest, though, that we keep the kids down there for the moment while a couple of us see what we can find out."

I called down the stairs for Tom and Bill to come up. We headed out onto the front lawn. The alarms were still silent, and I felt a little better. There was a bright reddish-orange glow off to the southeast, nothing like the incredibly brilliant light we had seen just a short while ago. but still frightening-looking. It appeared as though the flames of hell were just beyond the horizon. We could see what we thought might be the shadow of a mushroom cloud, although at that distance we could not be sure. Suddenly, I realized that Carter was talking with his men on the radio. "Carter! The radio! It worked!" He looked at me like I was going nuts, and then suddenly, realization dawned in his eyes.

"You're right! It worked! Oh, thank goodness, it worked!" By now, Tom and Bill were looking at both of us as if we were both headed off the deep end.

Tom had a puzzled look on his face. "So, what if the radio works...... OH! Does that mean that even if there was a nuclear detonation, there was no EMP?"

Carter smiled. "It appears that if that detonation caused an EMP, it either is not affecting us here, or else it was not big enough to interfere with smaller things like radios." He looked at the watch on his wrist. "I have a computerized watch, and it is still working, so I guess any EMP that may have occurred simply did not affect us."

"Do you think Homeland is done with its attack?" asked Bill. Carter looked thoughtful for a minute.

"I would hope so, but there is really no way to tell. I am going to try to get hold of the General to find where they are and see if he knows anything. Meanwhile, I need to go check on my folks on the outer berm. Let's plan to meet back here on the porch in an hour if nothing else happens. Keep your eyes peeled for drones or other aircraft, but let's stay off the radios for now if we can." Carter headed off towards the barracks, and I turned to Tom and Bill.

"I would feel a lot better if we kept everyone downstairs for a while until we knew something more. Let's wait until morning and if it looks clear, we can let people come up out of the basement and also get a few of the security cameras back on line then." Tom and Bill agreed with me, and Bill went back into the house to let everyone know to stay in the basement until morning. With nothing else to do, Tom and I sat on the front steps to wait for Carter to come back. The Nuk-Alerts remained silent, but I continued to feel a strong sense of foreboding. As the minutes passed, the feeling of foreboding continued to grow. After about 20 minutes, the feeling was so strong I could feel myself start to tremble. Tom must have sensed my distress because he put his arm around my shoulders.

"You're shaking. Are you cold?" I shook my head.

"No, I'm just...it's that feeling again. It's not over. Something is going to happen, and soon. I know Carter said to stay off the radio, but can you call him and see if he is on the way back?" Tom pulled the radio from his pocket and attempted to call Carter.

"I thought we put fresh batteries in the all the radios. This one is not coming on." Tom took the batteries out of the back of the radio and wiped them off before putting them back in and reassembling the radio. He continued to fiddle with the switches, but nothing seemed to make the radio come on. Suddenly he stopped and looked at me.

"It happened, didn't it. An EMP just hit us."

"We don't know that for sure, but that radio was working fine a half an hour ago. Is your watch still working?"

Tom grinned as he looked at his watch. "This watch is EMP proof. It belonged to my grandfather and it has no batteries in it – just a plain old wind-up-every-morning kind of watch." I looked at my wrist, and my watch had stopped. For some reason, that made me incredibly sad – as though life itself had just stopped. I could feel the tears starting to slip down my cheeks. Suddenly, I could not help myself and I was sobbing into Tom's shoulder. I don't think he expected that, because he started helplessly patting my back as I bawled. After a couple of minutes, he pulled his handkerchief out of his pocket and wiped my eyes and cheeks. I took a couple of deep breaths and pulled myself together.

"I'm sorry, Tom, I didn't mean to get so upset. It just seems that we can't catch a break. Everyone has been through so much already, and this is like the final straw. The power was out before, but it was because there was nobody willing to work for free to keep the power going. An EMP will destroy what was left of the grid, and it's going to put everyone back a hundred years or so. How will we ever get back to normal?" I was silent for a minute or two, and then Tom answered me.

"It's not really the final straw, just the end of our old way of life. This could be a beginning, if we can learn to have the right attitude. It is going to be up to us and to others like us all across the country if we ever want to get our America back. We just have to keep plugging away at fixing things. Please don't let this get you down. You've been so strong though all of this, don't give up now." It took a few minutes for me to get control of my tears, but eventually I took a deep breath, squared my shoulders, and turned to Tom.

"Thank you. You're right. We need to look at this as just another bump in the road. Right now, we need to find Carter. Until we know if our electronics that were supposed to be protected will work, we will need to post extra sentries on the outer berm, and we'll need to let our folks in the inner berm know what is going on. We'll need to keep watching for radiation, too. Let's see if the ATVs still work, and we can ride over there." Luckily, the ATVs were not computerized at all and were not affected by the EMP. We decided to swing by the foxholes on the inner berm first to check on everyone and let them know what we thought was happening. After a few quick words of reassurance with each of our folks, we headed over to Carter's RV.

We found Carter outside the RV talking with Mark and several of his officers. When he saw us coming, he waved us over to join their discussion.

"I was on the radio with the general when the EMP hit. Fortunately, we were almost done with our conversation when the radio went dead. The general and all but one group of his troops are accounted for and made it out of Bragg safely. He plans to be here tomorrow morning to meet with all of us. I don't know if the EMP will change that, but I don't expect that it will. General McPherson doesn't usually let little things like the collapse of the country or the total destruction of the grid faze him too much!" We all chuckled at Carter's unexpected humor.

"What do we need to do tonight to get ready for the general's visit tomorrow?" I asked. Carter looked thoughtful for a moment.

"We'll need to have a place to meet – the dining hall will do for that. I'll bring over a couple of large maps of the area, although I suspect he will bring his own. We need to be sure our sentries are on high alert, since we don't know if Homeland knows where the general is right now. Let's try to keep the kids and civilians out of the area – is it too much to ask them to stay away from the dining hall tomorrow morning?"

I looked at Tom and we both nodded. "That's a good idea," I said. "I think we can get the kitchen folks to make a quick and easy breakfast for everyone downstairs. We'll need to get a couple of cameras up and get at least some of the solar hooked back up before that, though. What else?"

"Let's keep the sentries doubled tomorrow – at least until we find out what the general's plans are. We also need to have someone watching for drones or planes. Can you be sure someone is in the OP to do that?" Carter frowned for a moment. "I'm not sure what else needs to be done tonight. Not knowing what time in the morning to expect the general, let's plan on getting together around seven. Do what you need to with the solar and cameras, and then try to get some rest. I'm sure the general will make sure tomorrow is a really busy day for all of us."

"We'll need to monitor for radiation during the night. You've got one of these fobs. The more radiation there is, the faster it chirps." Carter pulled the Nuk-Alert out of his pocket and looked at it, then put it back in his shirt pocket.

"Thanks. If we start hearing chirps, you need to get all your folks back down to the basement. My troops have some protection against radiation, and we will handle the security. At the first sign of radiation, pull your folks off the berm and get downstairs. I will hopefully see you both in the morning."

We said goodnight, and Tom and I headed back to the house. I gave Frank one of the Nuk-Alerts and explained to him how it worked. He agreed to keep monitoring and let the security teams know if they needed to take shelter because of radiation. Tom got Frank and Bill started on the hooking up a few of the cameras, while I got Kiara, Marty, and Tim busy checking the solar and hooking some of it back up. While they were busy, I shared Carter's information with the rest of the group. Jon and Chris both volunteered to take the day shift tomorrow in the OP. Several others volunteered to double up with the scheduled sentries in the fox holes. Once that was settled, I talked to Janet about breakfast. She thought it would be no problem to feed our folks in the house tomorrow if the soldiers could eat MREs instead of coming to the dining hall. I'm glad she mentioned that, because I had forgotten that Carter's group usually ate in the dining hall at mealtime. She also mentioned she would be sure there was a good supply of coffee ready while the general was here.

"Carter told me once that the general lives on coffee. I'll also make sure there are Danish or rolls or something to go with the coffee. We don't want the general to think he is visiting an apocalyptic refugee camp or anything!" Janet smiled as she headed over to talk to Maria and Gabby. Knowing those three, I knew I did not need to worry about breakfast for the general in the morning.

Tom and I headed back over to Carter's RV to remind him about his troops' breakfast, and he nodded.

"Thanks for thinking of that. I already gave instructions to my troops that breakfast would be MREs. I want them ready for the general at six. I don't know what time he'll be here, but I am betting on early. I think it will be a good morale booster for everyone if he comes and sees that we can still act like a functional combat unit. It will be good for the troops, too. They need to see they have an important role to play in the battles I know are coming. And... I think it will be good for you and for your folks to see that we are ready to deal with anything that might come along. One of the things the general is fond of saying is that the optics are important. How things look can influence people's attitude." Carter paused a moment, and then looked at Tom and me. "I want you two front and center when the general arrives. You are such an important part of why we are as ready as we are. Of course, I don't expect either of you to be in uniform, though." He chuckled as we looked at him in surprise. We talked for a few minutes more, then headed back to the house. I wanted to find Kiara to see if she thought the solar would work after the EMP. Tom said he would check on the cameras and make sure the generators would work in the morning. Then, hopefully a couple of hours of sleep and, I hope, no nightmares.

CHAPTER TWO

General Wayne McPherson sat with his elbows on the cluttered table. The single light bulb hanging from the peak of his tent cast shadows across his face, making him look much older than his fifty-eight years. He reached up to rub his tired eyes and took a sip of his cold cup of coffee. "Sammy, have you heard from Major Angelo's group yet?"

Colonel Samuel Iverson checked the list in his hand and answered, "I'm sorry, Mac, no contact with them yet."

The general shook his head wearily. "I hope they got out. They were the last group to leave, and we should have heard from them by now."

"I expect it will take them a while to get somewhere that they feel safe calling in. We also have to consider that their radios might have been damaged if they were close enough for the EMP effect from the nuke. In any case, at least we've heard from all of the other teams. How in the world did you know they were going to attack Bragg? Was it all the stuff Carter was worried about that set you off?"

"No, I just figured it would make strategic sense for them to try to take out our headquarters. Thankfully, when I talked to the Joint Chiefs two weeks ago, they told me the same thing. I'm not surprised that Carter thought of it, though."

Sammy laughed. "Yeah, I was kind of surprised to hear him talking about having a bad feeling. He didn't strike me as a psychic kind of guy, you know? Turns out he was right about those Homeland traitors, though."

"Yeah, I thought he was nuts at first, talking about gut feelings, but he has a real talent for anticipating tactical scenarios. Not to mention, my own gut was screaming the same thing. That's why I started the evacuations when I did. I just hope we did enough, that we got everyone out in time. I just wish we would hear from Angelo and his troops."

"If he got out, you know he will contact you. I can think of at least ten scenarios where he got out but is unable to call to check in. Knowing him, he is probably trying to do damage assessment from the nuke."

"He'd better not be." replied the general. "I don't think he has the equipment to do that safely, and it really doesn't matter what they did to Bragg. We're done there. Tomorrow, we're going to see Carter at his location. It sounds like he lucked out when he found that farm. He might have some insights for us about the area I've chosen to establish our next base. These caves are great for hiding and I'm glad we found out about them, but they are also damp, dark, and cold, and I don't relish staying here very long." He rubbed his hand across his eyes and finished the last sip of cold coffee. Sammy looked at the general, worry etched across his face.

"Mac, why don't you try to get some rest. I'm going to go check on the men standing watch, and then I'll be back. It will be dawn in a couple of hours, and time to head over to Carter's."

"I can't. I've got too much to do. I'll sleep when I'm dead, I guess. I'm still working up our plans for tomorrow. Just bring me another cup of coffee when you head back this way, okay?"

Sammy smiled at the general. "What are you going to do when we all run out of coffee?"

General McPherson faked a frown at his friend and barked, "Do not even think about that. Do not talk about that. It will be a tragic day when that happens. No coffee? That will really be the end of the world as we know it."

Sammy laughed as he exited the tent. No coffee will indeed be the end of civilization! Of course, he thought, civilization is already pretty fleeting. If people told him a year ago that Homeland forces would conduct a nuke attack on American soil, he'd swear they were nuts and that their tin foil hats were on too tight. But, it happened, and he still couldn't believe it.

After Sammy left, General McPherson picked up his radio and contacted Carter to let him know that they were headed out to his area in the morning. After only about three minutes of conversation, though, the radio quit working, the noisy generator became silent, and the light hanging in his tent slowly faded. McPherson stood, pulling the flashlight from his belt and switching it on. "Thank goodness this still works," he muttered. He walked out of the tent to see Sammy rushing towards him, flashlight in one hand and coffee pot in the other.

"General," he called, "I do believe we were just hit with an EMP!"

"Well, Sammy, I'm glad you have your priorities right and brought the coffee with you. Leave the coffee here and chill a little. Can't have the troops seeing you look so distressed – after all, optics are important. When you can, go double the watches for tonight, and then come back. We have some work to do." The General turned and went back into the tent. He sat back down at the table and propped his flashlight up to shed light over the maps he had spread out. A few minutes later, Sammy came back carrying a larger lantern, which he placed on the table. The general smiled his thanks and moved the lantern closer to his maps.

"I am not surprised at all that they set off an EMP after they destroyed Fort Bragg – assuming it was Homeland who did it. The more they cripple the country, the easier it will be for Homeland to take over and set up their anti-Constitutional government. The thing is, though, that Homeland has not taken a few things into consideration. First of all, it is not good strategy to piss off a general who is overtired and has not had enough coffee. Second, I do not think the American people will appreciate this at all, and this may be just the impetus needed to get those militias all fired up. Third, I don't think Homeland realizes we have hardened a lot of our equipment over the last couple of months. Yes, we probably lost the generators that were running, but we have more in the back of the caves. Most of our vehicles should still work, and we have a lot of other electronics that were protected. To be honest with you, I really expected the EMP to happen weeks ago. Which brings me to our plan. What do you know about the town of Riverdale?"

Sammy shrugged his shoulders. "Not much, sir. I know that Carter says it has been hit really hard by a number of things including a lot of violence from a renegade motorcycle gang. I also know that Carter sent information about a possible sleeper group in the area trying to damage the railroad. He also said that the farm where he is staying right now is very well organized and is doing well. As far as resources, I know there is the railroad, a branch of a good-sized river runs through the town, and there is a community airport. Other than that, I really do not have any additional information."

"OK, come look at the map. I notice that there is a private college campus here alongside the airport. I doubt if there are any classes going on, and so we are going to go back to school. I think that would make an excellent place to set up shop. Get a couple of squads to go out now and do some recon. In the morning, I want the airport and the campus secured for us to move in by 1400. Tell your troops if there are peaceful civilians living on the campus or at the airport, they are not to hassle them. I'll deal with them when I get there tomorrow. We will help them relocate to a safe and secure area. On the other hand, if they find gang members or anyone hostile to Patriot soldiers, they should place them under arrest until I get there."

"Are we going to set up permanently in Riverdale, then?"

"Ah, I wish I could say it was permanent. We are going to establish a base of operations there. The war that we are fighting, though, will be very fluid. It's not like we can just go bomb the daylights out of the enemy and his territory, because interspersed among the enemy are American citizens. We need to protect them. We also want to keep as much of the infrastructure intact as we can, so we can recover from this when it's all over. So, we'll set up our command elements in Riverdale and then move out from there. First step is to get settled and make contact with Carter's group. Second step is to find the sleeper cell in Riverdale and take them out. Third, we fortify this area so we can expand. We need to create safe places for civilians to live, too, like they did at the farm."

Sammy gave a low whistle. "Sounds like we have our work cut out for us, then. What time will we leave to go see Carter?"

"I'd like to leave here around dawn. Have Major Stein and Major Phillips secure this area and be ready to move to the airport when we return. Also, have Lieutenant Evans get some of the men to check the equipment in the back of the caves to be sure it all still works. I plan to leave a small contingent of men to protect the large equipment in the caves until we are ready to move it. Then, when all that is done, please go get some rest. Tomorrow will be a really busy day."

Sammy saluted and left the tent. After he was gone, the general poured himself another cup of coffee and went back to studying the maps.

It seemed like I just closed my eyes when I woke up to see it was already five AM. I quickly got up, washed my face, brushed my teeth and got dressed. I came upstairs to find Tom already up, sitting in my office and drinking a cup of tea. He reached over the desk and handed me a steaming cup.

"I don't hear the generators – does that mean the solar is working?" I asked.

"Well, we really won't know until after the sun comes out," Tom said, smiling.

"Well, duh, that was a stupid question, wasn't it? Guess I'm not all that awake yet," I answered, embarrassed by my question.

Tom smiled back at me. "Kiara tested all of the photo-voltaic panels. As best we can tell, we only lost one panel and Kiara was able to replace it. That woman is an electrical wizard! So far, the system seems to be working without any issues. We ran the generators for a while last night to get the batteries all charged up. Kiara checked out all of the components and so far, everything seems to be operational. That's a relief." Tom must have noticed I was feeling a little preoccupied, because he changed the topic. "Are you ready for the general's visit this morning?"

"I think so. I am a little concerned that he will want to take over the farm. That's not going to happen, but he can set up on adjoining property if he wants. I'm a little nervous about that, though, because I don't want us to become an even bigger target." I sipped my tea, and Tom reached over to take my hand.

"Let's not worry about things before they happen, OK? Let's just meet the general, hear what he has to say, and then go from there. Like my mother used to say, don't borrow trouble." I squeezed Tom's hand, grinned at him, and put my teacup down. "Okay, then, let's go find Carter."

We found Carter outside his RV talking with several of his officers. As we approached, his officers saluted him, turned, and went towards the barracks buildings.

"Good morning! Any word from the general yet?" I asked.

"Good morning. No word yet, but I expect he should be here soon. I sent my officers in to round up the troops and get them into formation, so we are ready when he arrives. I've got spotters out on the road who will let us know when they see his entourage approaching."

"That's a smart idea. Do we have any kind of agenda for his visit? Or will he just come in and tell us what we have to do?" I think Carter could tell I was a little nervous about what the general might be planning.

"Please don't worry about what he wants to do. He recognizes all of the hard work you all have done, and I guarantee he won't do anything to jeopardize that. In the couple of conversations I've had with him since I got here, he has been extremely complimentary and very impressed with how well you guys thought out everything. I'm betting that more than anything, he will want to pick your brains for ways to get Riverdale set up as well."

I was about to reply when Carter's radio squealed. He spoke briefly into the radio and then looked at us and said, "The general and his staff are about 20 minutes out." He pulled out a small air horn from his pocket and sounded three sharp blasts. Immediately, soldiers began to pour out of the barracks and line up in formation on the pasture next to the barracks. I was surprised at how sharp the troops looked, in spite of not having access to irons, starch or even real laundry facilities. As I watched the troops, I was amused to see the squad of Marines off to the side in their own formation. As everyone fell into place, I was impressed to see each company even had guidon flags with unit designations posted. Tom and I stood off to the side of the formation and watched as the officers made sure everything was perfect. I have to admit that Tom and I both were enjoying the military pomp and ceremony, and I was even feeling a bit nostalgic for the days when I, too, would have been a part of the formation.

Suddenly, the officers began to issue commands, echoed by the platoon sergeants, to come to attention. Tom and I both straightened up, too, and looked towards the gate as several Humvees pulled through. As the Humvees parked, several soldiers got out of each one. The soldiers all took places in front and behind a person I assumed was the general. While Carter was greeting the general and his staff, I took a moment to study the man who would most likely influence the course of our future. General McPherson was rather tall, about 6'3". He had dark cropped hair with significant grey at the temples. Even from a distance I could see that he had a weathered, tired face, but he was smiling as he looked over the formation of troops in front of him. He was accompanied by a slightly shorter man with steely grey hair and dark eyes. I assumed this was Colonel Iverson, the general's adjutant.

After greeting the general and his staff, Carter invited General McPherson to review his troops. I loved watching this – there is something very comforting about watching the timeless traditions of the military. I know that George Washington probably used the same ceremonies to review his troops as we were seeing today and, God willing, a hundred years from now, American troops would still be reviewed the same way. With everything in the world so unstable right now, the continuity of the familiar routines helped us feel a sense of safety and security.

After reviewing the troops, the general addressed the men and women standing before him.

"Soldiers...oh, and Marines," he began, with a grin to the platoon of Marines standing separately from everyone else.

"Ooorah," the Marines shouted in response, bringing a smile to everyone's face.

"At ease, everyone. My name is General Wayne McPherson, and by order of the Joint Chiefs, I am now the commander of all Patriot troops in the Southeastern United States. I answer directly to the Joint Chiefs and to the lawful President of this country. I am here today for several reasons. The most important reason is to share information with you. I am not sure how much access you all have had to information on what is going on in the country, so let me try to explain what has been happening. As many of you know, our economy was sliding downward in spite of the efforts of some, including the President, to improve jobs, increase the spending power of the dollar, and reduce taxes. Unfortunately, a small, highly partisan group of politicians did everything they could to disrupt and sabotage those efforts. I have it on good authority that not only did those radical partisans cause the downturn of the economy, they also arranged the acts of terrorism that became the final straw to totally collapse the economy and the country. At this time, about 95 per cent of the military remains under the control of the Joint Chiefs. The five percent that chose not to align themselves with the Joint Chiefs, and by extension the Constitution, instead are now part of Homeland Security and they are actively fighting against our troops. The United Nations was invited by the partisans to provide troops to act as supposed peacekeepers. They are in most of the big cities in the Northeastern states and in California. As of now, they have not been involved in any combat operations, and we do not know if that will change or not.

"After the economy collapsed, the President enacted the Continuity of Government plan which called for all members of the congress, the cabinet, and others to move to select safe locations so that the work of the government could continue uninterrupted. Unfortunately, members of the radical partisans infiltrated these locations, and as the designated people arrived at each location, they were taken prisoner and held hostage. We have been able to free some of these people, but in the process, there was significant fighting. I am sorry to say that some of these people were injured or killed in the process. As of right now, as best as we can tell the President is alive but is still being held hostage.

"As most of you know, sometime last night, Fort Bragg was bombed and an EMP was set off. We suspect this was done to try to beat us all down to make it easier for these radicals to take over. I think, though, that as we get the word out to the American public and do our best to help each other, the opposite will happen and we – both military and citizens – will become stronger together.

"We have all been through a difficult time, and I am sorry to say it is going to get harder before it gets better. The America we all know and love, the country all of us serve and that many of us have fought and bled for, that country is in danger of being lost. The traitors at the top of our government who are attempting to overthrow the legitimate government of the United States of America want to implement their radical vision of America. Their vision is not the vision of our founding fathers, and it does not include the Constitution we hold dear. They have a vision of a Socialist state, where there is no reward for hard work and no room for personal initiative. They do not respect all of our rights under the Constitution – in fact, they do not believe in the Constitution. Their heroes are not our heroes. While most of us respect and admire people who worked hard to protect the rights and freedoms of all people, their heroes are people who I consider to have oppressed people for political or personal gain.

"I've heard a lot of talk and arguing among troops over the last few months blaming all of this on the Democrats and all of the liberals. That is not exactly true. There are many people who are Democrats or who have a liberal point of view who do not support or condone the actions of these radical traitors. We must not paint all Democrats or liberals with the same brush. We need to keep in mind that our country is based on the concept of respectful discourse. We need to have people with contrasting opinions; after all, that is what free speech is all about. The enemy is trying to divide us, and we cannot let that happen. Our strength is in all of us standing together.

"We are now beginning a new phase of the effort to take our country back. We need to engage *all* citizens, not just the conservative right. We need to remember people are (or at least should be) Americans first and partisans second. Over the next few weeks, we will have multiple missions. Yes, we will be fighting the illegal and radical forces of Homeland, but we will also be working to restore towns across the country, to help our citizens regain their freedoms and a safe and satisfying way of life. That means all citizens, not just the ones with whom you may share ideologies. Some of you will be tasked with helping to rebuild homes and businesses. Others will be helping citizens learn to survive and regain a productive living. Some of you will be tasked with fighting Homeland forces and with helping train local militias to be able to fight alongside of you. Regardless of your assignments, *all* of you will be vital members of our battle to take back America.

"The United States has always been a shining beacon to the rest of the world. Our goal is simple. Keep that light of liberty burning. Abraham Lincoln once said, 'America will never be destroyed from the outside. If we falter and lose our freedoms, it will be because we destroyed ourselves.' Our mission is to be sure we do not allow people within our country to destroy our freedoms or our nation. I guarantee this will not be easy. Some of us may get hurt, and some of us may die. All of us will need to make sacrifices. I pray none makes the ultimate sacrifice, but we must acknowledge that is a possibility. We are not being paid to serve, and none of us will become materially wealthy as a result of this conflict. However, we will regain our country. We will regain our freedom, our heritage, and our rights as citizens of the greatest nation on the face of the planet Earth, and **that** is wealth beyond measure.

"If you do not share the goal of restoring America to be the nation it was intended to be or if you are not willing to participate in this historic battle, now would be a good time for you to leave. I will remind you, though, of something Samuel Adams once said. 'If ye love wealth better than liberty, the tranquility of servitude better than the animating contest of freedom, go home from us in peace. We ask not your counsels or your arms. Crouch down and lick the hands which feed you. May your chains set lightly upon you, and may posterity forget that you were our countrymen." I ask you now, will you be licking your masters' hands, or will you fight for America and your fellow citizens? Are you ready to take America back?" The men and women standing in formation gave a mighty roar, cheering the general, and chanting "USA, USA".

Once the troops settled down, the general continued. "We are reorganizing the military to be able to cope with the challenges being thrust upon us. One thing we had to do was suspend the Goldwater-Nichols Act of 1986 to give controlling authority to the Joint Chiefs. With troops scattered around the world, we have had to re-arrange command structure. As a result, I am promoting several people and giving them additional responsibilities. COL Carter Murphy, you are being promoted to Brigadier General, and you will have responsibility for all special forces troops in the southeastern United States. Captain Mark Schmidt, you are being promoted to Major, and you will have the responsibility of this garrison and specific civilian components. COL Samuel Iverson, I am promoting you to Brigadier General, and you will be responsible for the garrison in Riverdale."

The three men stepped forward, and the general called all soldiers to attention. He stepped in front of Carter, and said, "Attention to orders. The President of the United States and the Joint Chiefs of Staff have reposed special trust and confidence in your patriotism, valor, fidelity and abilities. In view of these qualities and your demonstrated potential for increased responsibility, you are, therefore, promoted in the United States Army to the grade of Brigadier General." He then reached over and removed the colonel insignia from Carter's collar and replaced it with a single star. After exchanging salutes, the ceremony was repeated for both COL Iverson and Mark. The general then presented the three newly promoted officers to the troops.

After a few minutes of enthusiastic cheering, Carter called his troops to attention and dismissed them. He and Mark then escorted General McPherson and BG Iverson over to where we were standing and introduced us to the two men. I complimented the general on his rousing call to arms and told him I thought he greatly inspired not only the troops, but Tom and me as well.

"Thank you, Denise. I want to keep our troops energized and engaged in this battle. It is going to be hard, and their only rewards will be to regain their country. I also feel really strongly that it is going to take everyone, not just the right wing, to regain our country and put it back together the way it was intended to be. I want them to start thinking of all of us as a team, not as members of one political party or the other. Heaven knows, when this is all over, I hope we can develop new parties that are not as adversarial as Republicans and Democrats. That is why we never seemed to get anything done in the past – everyone was too busy sniping at the other side. Now, we need to only snipe at the group of traitors who are holding this country hostage."

Tom and I nodded our agreement with the general. He made a good point about working together. We chatted for a few more minutes, and then took our guests on a tour of the farm. General McPherson was impressed with our double berms, especially that the inner berm was completely made of conexes used for storage. We took him by each of the foxholes and introduced him to our people who were on duty. Then, as we headed towards the house, we made a stop at the Observation Post (OP). Chris and Jon were in the OP, and, of course, the general had to climb up and check out the view. I was proud of my sons, because when one was talking to the general, the other was maintaining his watch for drones or other aircraft. After the OP, we stopped at the barn and introduced Clark, Maureen, and the girls. Then, a quick stop to the infirmary so the general could meet James, Lionel, Samantha, and Amy, and then we went over to the dining hall. Janet, Maria, and Gabby outdid themselves. Not only was there a large commercial pot of coffee ready, there was also a platter of breakfast burritos and pastries. On the far wall, Carter had mounted a large map of the area, and a table was set up in front of the map.

We invited our guests to fix themselves plates, and we did the same. As we sat down at the table, I found myself sitting next to General McPherson, with Carter on his other side. Tom, Mark, and BG Iverson sat on the other side of the table. We continued with polite cultural chit-chat over breakfast. After the general finished eating and poured himself another cup of coffee, he stood and walked over to the map.

"I must say, I am quite impressed with the way you all have organized this farm. Your security looks to be quite good, and you seem to have the resources needed for survival. I want to reassure you that I am not planning anything that would impact your safety or ability to survive. Let me explain to you what my plan is and how I hope you all will be able to help.

"First of all, let me give you some history. Before all of this started, I was the commanding officer for the United States Army Special Operations Command at Fort Bragg. My responsibilities included oversight of the Special Forces Command; the 75th Ranger Regiment; the Special Warfare School; Civil Affairs, Sustainment, and Military Information Brigades; and the Special Operations Aviation Command. About three months before the coup took place, we started hearing rumors of impending action. At the time, we did not know exactly what was being planned, but several of us in Command roles at Bragg got together to do some 'just in case' planning. We felt pretty sure that the extremists on the left were going to try something to overthrow the lawful government. We did not know what they would do, but the signs all pointed to an attempt at a coup coming soon. We hoped we were wrong, but all of us knew deep down we were right. We decided to try to exfiltrate troops and a lot of supplies and equipment to surrounding areas with support from the Joint Chiefs. One of my officers grew up in this general area and was forever talking about the caverns around his home. We decided the caverns would be a great place to temporarily hide a lot of supplies and equipment. We set up some supposed training missions for some of our special forces troops as a cover to get the equipment out of Bragg and hidden from sight.

"When the actual take-over in Washington happened, we knew we would have to get out of Bragg sooner rather than later. We found many reasons to move troops from both Bragg and Pope Air Field. We also moved many of the military families to other bases where we felt they would be safer. When I found out who the general was who was calling the shots for Homeland forces on the east coast, I knew we were in trouble. I've known him for a long time, and he hates me – mostly for personal reasons. That made my gut scream that Bragg would be targeted. By the time we heard rumors of impending action, we actually did not have that many troops or that much equipment left. We had already sent out a lot of the 18th Airborne Corps and the 82nd Infantry Division via planes. The 82nd for now is at Fort Campbell, Kentucky, and the 18th Airborne Corps went to Fort Bliss, Texas. At the same time, we put out word to the civilian population of the surrounding towns to evacuate.

"I have a number of special forces troops out working with local militias all across the mid-Atlantic states, as far north as Pennsylvania, and down to South Carolina. As the different militias become trained and ready, the troops move on to train the next group in an expanding circle. Eventually, we hope there will be enough trained militias to fight side by side with our soldiers and Marines and to hold the lines.

"I've decided to establish a base of operations in Riverdale. It makes sense to me for many reasons, too many to go into right now. My men are clearing the airport and the college campus next door to the airport, and that is where we are going to set up. I also want to establish a secure location for the citizens of Riverdale. There does not seem to be too many people left, but many may be in hiding. Carter, I believe you've had your men out looking at various places where we can create a secure community. Have they found anything yet?"

"Yes, actually we found a neighborhood close to the college campus that will need some work but is defensible and can accommodate quite a few families. There is a small school and strip mall in this neighborhood. Although all of the stores have been trashed, I believe we could repair them enough to use them to eventually get some degree of trade going." Carter walked over to the map and began pointing. "I circled the neighborhood on the map so you can see where it is in relation to the farm and to the airport and college."

"Excellent. Mark, I am putting you in charge of refurbishing this community. Let Carter know what you will need, and he will arrange it. The sooner we have the citizens taken care of, the sooner we can start putting things back together. Mark, your troops will continue to stay in their barracks at the farm and will have several responsibilities. Security of the farm is paramount. I expect some will also help with the community restoration project. Carter, you can headquarter at the farm or at the Riverdale complex, which ever works for you. Your troops are spread out across the map, but you will need to have a safe place for them when they come back from missions. I suspect you would be better off at the Riverdale complex where there is a lot more room." Carter nodded his acknowledgment.

The general then turned to BG Iverson. "Sammy, I want you to get with the troops we brought. I want a couple of companies assigned to security for our new base. I also want you to put together a team to go after the sleeper cell that tried to destroy the rail lines and any other sleepers around. You will need to handle the logistics for the Riverdale garrison. We have most of our sustainment brigade with us, I believe, and so they will need to set up warehouses for supplies, a medical area, food service, housing, motor pool, armory, communications, and all the other things we need to keep our work going. I will be getting our aviation folks squared away and working with the Air Force to get their people out here too."

I cleared my throat. "What about us, General? How can we help?"

"I was hoping you would ask that. I would like your people to help get our citizens settled, and to help train them. I'm sure Mark will need the help of all of your carpenters, plumbers, electricians, and such to get the new community refurbished. We want the citizens of Riverdale to see not just military, but citizens as well helping to rebuild. My goal is that as soon as the community is finished and people have moved in, we will start fixing up the next community, and so on. We may eventually bring some of the military families here that we moved to other bases. I know that will help our troops' morale immensely."

Tom jumped in and said, "Mark, you know as a contractor, I've got a great crew already at the farm. We will be more than happy to help with the actual construction. We still have a lot of the heavy equipment for dozing and well-drilling, and we can probably find a lot more solar equipment so that the new community can also have power and running water."

Mark nodded thoughtfully. "I can have my group of Marines do more scavenging for those kinds of supplies. If you can make a list of the supplies you think you may need for water, septic, and power, we can get them out looking right away." Tom pulled a pen and notepad from his pocket and began making a list.

I was excited that it looked as though we were going to revitalize the area, but I still had questions for which I needed answers. "General, I understand your focus is getting set up around here, but I still have some questions. First, if 95% of the military is on our side, who is fighting for Homeland? How close are the Homeland and UN troops? I understand there was some conflict in Northern Virginia. Has that been resolved? Will you be able to provide any defense to this area from aerial threats? How many troops do you have with you? Will you have planes or helicopters to help? How are you going to feed all of your troops? Do you think we will see combat in this area?"

"Whoa, hold on! One at a time. First, Homeland Security is made up of a number of agencies, including ICE, Border Patrol, the Coast Guard, FEMA, the Secret Service and the Transportation Security Administration."

"Oh, great," I snickered. "The TSA will fight us by throwing luggage at us, right."

General McPherson smiled and continued. "Homeland also has a large number of contractors – essentially mercenaries who will fight for pay. They do have a rather formidable force. The UN troops are mostly in the northeastern big cities - New York, Baltimore, Washington, Philadelphia, and so on. We know there are some homeland troops up around the Fairfax, Virginia area. The conflict that occurred was just outside Manassas. In fact, we are calling it "Third Manassas" in honor of the two battles there from the First Civil War that preceded this one. While we were able to push the Homeland forces back to Alexandria, the area is still very volatile.

We have several groups of Rangers up there working with the local Militia to hold our lines and we believe at least for now, they are being successful. Once we are set up, we have aviation elements I am working with that will move here. We'll have cargo planes and helicopters mostly at first, although once we lengthen the runways, we hope to accommodate fighters, too. Right now, the airport main runway is only 5500 feet long. We need to add at least another 500 feet to be able to accommodate the fighters. The second runway is a lot shorter, and we will probably just use that for the helicopters and small planes. As for air defense, yes, we have antiaircraft weapons, and once my Air Force buddies get here, they will be setting up additional radar and defensive capabilities. As for soldiers, all together I have somewhere around 1200 soldiers here with us, although I've not had time to take a head count. Many are special forces troops, but there are also others from Fort Bragg, plus our sustainment troops.

"What else did you ask? Oh, yes, food. We were able to get a significant amount of food stores hidden in the caverns in the weeks before the attack, so for now we will be fine – rations will be tight, but we have enough for quite a while. We will also be scavenging, and hopefully working with the local farms that might still be functioning to grow additional crops. Our sustainment troops will also be planting a large garden on the college campus, so we can supplement stored food with fresh.

"Finally, your question about combat here: I honestly do not know. I certainly hope not, but it all depends on the will of the UN troops to engage in battle with American troops. I've heard there are almost three million UN troops on the west coast and close to that many on the northeastern coast. Right now, we are not in any position to take on that many troops, but as our units around the country get coordinated, our chances at defeating them improve. We are trying to keep any combat localized to areas where these troops are already established. Any other questions?"

Tom raised his hand, and asked, "How about the president, senators and congressmen that were being held hostage? What's the story there?"

"We have been able to free a number of the hostages at this point, and they are in hiding. The President is still being held, but the Vice President is now free. As I mentioned to the troops, there was fighting involved in freeing these people, and unfortunately, that means that some hostages were injured, and a few were killed. All of the Joint Chiefs are free as well, and they are the ones coordinating all of the military actions across the country. I think that is all I'd better say about that at this point."

I could not resist asking, "In your talk to the troops today, you really hit it hard about not painting all liberals and democrats the same. What's the story with that?" The General paused and looked thoughtful before answering.

"I have had troops actually fight with each other – physically fight - over the schism between the left and the right. Both sides have valid points, and we can't condemn everyone for the actions of a few power-hungry radicals. I am tired of hearing people labeled because of the way they vote. I am fed up with both parties. Neither party has stepped up over the past few years to put an end to the troubles plaguing this nation. It could have been a simple fix if both sides would have worked together – but their individual interests were more important than the interests of the people of this country. I have soldiers in my command from both parties and they *all* love their country. The people who are causing this mess are not Democrats or Republicans. They are radical anti-Americans, and they are the ones who are the enemy to everything for which this country stands. I meant every word of what I said to those troops. We will not survive as a nation if we cannot have respectful discussions and disagreements. After all, it's through discussion and even disagreements that we come up with new and better ways to do things." He paused for a minute or two, and then looked at us somewhat sheepishly. "Forgive me for getting on my soapbox about this, but it is a topic about which I have strong feelings. We have got to close the gap, and in some ways, that is the mission that drives me. Remember Lincoln's speech about a house divided – we will not endure if this divide is not healed quickly."

I nodded agreement. The general's philosophy was different than what I had been thinking, but it did make sense. I would have to give this more thought later on. We continued to talk for a few more minutes, and then the general looked at his watch.

"Sammy, I think it is time we got back, especially if we plan on moving by 1400. Denise, Tom, it was a pleasure to meet both of you. I am sure we will be seeing each other soon. Carter, will you show us back to the gate?" We all shook hands, and Carter, Sammy, and the general left. Mark stayed behind and asked us to stay and talk for a few minutes. I thought that was a good idea, as we had a lot of work ahead of us. After Carter and our guests left, I patted Mark on the shoulder and said, "We are so proud of you! Wait until your parents hear about your promotion and new responsibilities. We'll do anything we can to support your new mission."

Mark smiled and said, "Thanks. I wanted to talk to the two of you about how we can go about fixing up this community. I have some ideas, but I wanted to hear what you both thought as well. After all, look at what you've done here."

Tom asked, "What kind of things are you wanting to hear from us?"

"Anything that will help us quickly and efficiently get this community going. The faster we get this done, the faster we can get people moved in and the faster we can work on getting us all back to whatever will pass for our new normal." Mark smiled and pointed at me. "You are the brainy one among the three of us. What are you thinking?"

I shook my head and rolled my eyes at him, pausing for a minute to think. "Can we go with you to get a look at this area? I think no matter what we do to get the homes fixed up, we need to focus on security of the area first. I don't know if there are enough conexes left to create a berm like we have here, but maybe we can find something else to create some kind of barrier to prevent people just walking in. We also need to be sure it is big enough that it doesn't feel like a jail to the people living there. I think our first priority should be making sure it is secure."

Mark nodded thoughtfully. "The community is a gated community, surrounded by a ten-foot wrought iron fence. We could probably do something to strengthen the fence itself. We did repair the gates, and we can put a guard shack in at the gate as well."

I was excited to hear there already was a fence. "Having a fence already in place is great. That should save us some time. We probably ought to have a squad walk the fence to be sure it is intact and that nobody has knocked any of it down. Once we know the area is reasonably secure, we can start fixing up homes, one block at a time. Once we have a block ready, we can start moving people in and they can help getting the next block ready. I think people need to help create their own neighborhoods or else they will start to have an entitlement mentality, and heaven knows we will not be providing everything for these people. They will have to plant their own gardens and figure out how to get items they need by trading or bartering. I suppose we will need to teach them how to plant unless we get some farmers or gardeners in the group. I also think we need to think about where wells need to be placed, and where septic tanks can be installed if homes don't already have them. We need to have a map with everything on it – homes, sheds, sewer lines, water lines, all that kind of stuff."

Mark started laughing. I looked at him to see if he was losing his mind or what. He tried to stop laughing, and said, "You are the only person I know who is so OCD that in the midst of a national disaster, you want maps with all the details. You said all that and didn't even stop to take a breath. But, you are correct that it would be very helpful to have those details, especially when we go to dig wells and try to get running water. Tom, do you think we could get a couple of large wells established and hook up to the existing water lines?"

"I think we need to check out what's there before I answer that. Can we take a run over there tomorrow?"

"Sure. Let me get a few folks together to come with us for security, and we can go around seven o'clock, if that's okay with both of you. I'll be leaving a few troops there to provide security. Why don't you meet us over by the barracks at seven? Oh, and make sure you are both armed."

"Works for us," Tom said. With that, we said our goodbyes and headed back to the house. We were met at the door by a crowd, all wanting to know what we learned from the general. We suggested everyone come out onto the porch. Once everyone interested was settled, we proceeded to tell everyone what we learned about Homeland forces, about the general and his plans, and what our role would be in helping the area recover. We also told everyone about the promotions and Mark and Carter's new responsibilities. I could see a lot of smiles and nods of agreement as Tom and I talked about renovating the community and finding townspeople to move into the secured areas.

"Tom and I will be going with Mark and a few troops into the area tomorrow to see what we have to work with. I'll bring my tablet, so I can take pictures to show you all later. Once we know what's there, we'll figure out who is going to do what. Mark will give us some of his troops to help with labor and security. He is also sending the Marines out to start scavenging things we'll need for the construction in the area. Let's plan on meeting tonight after dinner and we can start making plans then."

Everyone seemed to be agreeable to that, and so Tom and I headed to the kitchen to grab a sandwich before we got busy with today's tasks. Frank and Bill followed us into the kitchen, both with serious expressions. Frank spoke first. "I'm worried that if we have people leaving from here to work in the community, we won't have enough help here for everything, especially security."

Bill added, "Yes, especially since we have so many acres of freshly planted fields to guard, and all the kids."

I looked at Tom and he answered, "Guys, we are going to help, but we won't be the only ones there working. Most of the actual labor will be done by the troops. We will not let that many people leave the area at a time. Carter and the general both assured us Mark's men will continue to provide security for the farm. We will have specialists going to help – Kiara, Marty, Jose, Tim, Red, and I will be providing electrical, plumbing, and construction oversight. Denise will be helping to find people to put into these neighborhoods, but she won't be going anywhere alone or unarmed. There will be security at the site, too. I appreciate your concern, and at the first sign our security is lacking, we will pull back on the project."

I added, "We have been incredibly lucky here that we are able to have as many people living comfortably here as we do. Who knows what the townspeople have been dealing with. This is our chance to help our neighbors regain some of the quality of life we already have." Frank and Bill nodded in agreement. I echoed Tom's promise that we would not let this project get in the way of our security here.

"I'm sure you all have tons of things to do – I know I do. We need to check all of our equipment, radios, and other things to see if anything was damaged by the EMP. I also need to find some folks and thank them for breakfast!"

CHAPTER THREE

I headed back over to the community kitchen in the dining hall and found Janet, Gabby, and Maria putting away the last of the cleaned dishes from breakfast.

"Ladies, you really impressed the General and his adjutant. Actually, I think you really knocked their socks off. Thank you so much for all of the extra effort you three put in this morning."

The three smiled, and Janet spoke up. "We wanted the general to see that we are able to survive here, and we can teach the other townspeople to survive, too. We figured if we could show our stuff to the general, he might have more confidence in all of our ability to overcome all of these challenges."

Maria chimed in, "Plus, it is our chance to do something for the soldiers who are helping us, protecting us, and who might be saving us."

I gave each of the three hugs. When I hugged Gabby, though, I noticed she looked really uncomfortable. On closer look, I noticed her hands and feet were puffy and even her face looked a bit swollen.

"Are you OK, dear?" I asked.

Gabby gave a weak smile. "Yes, I just don't feel really good. I'm sure it is just being so pregnant and all of the stress of the EMP and everything, but I have a splitting headache."

I told her to go lay down, and that I was going to go find James and Maureen to come check her over. Maria took her by the arm and offered to walk with her to her room. After they left, Janet told me she tried to get Gabby to go back to bed, but she insisted on helping make breakfast for everyone. "I think she is really overdoing it, and she still has a few more weeks before the baby is due. She really needs to take it easy. Maria and I can manage and if we need help, we can get one of the others to jump in." I agreed with Janet and left to go find James and Maureen.

An hour later, James, Maureen, Gabby and I were in Jon and Gabby's bedroom as Jon burst through the door.

"Gabby, honey, are you okay? What's going on? Is the baby okay?" he asked, looking frantic. I put my arm around Jon and told him to settle down, that both mom and baby would be okay. Jon sat on the bed next to Gabby and held her hand. She smiled at him and reassured him she would be fine. Jon looked at James and asked him what was wrong.

James explained he and Maureen had examined Gabby and thought she might be starting to show signs of pre-eclampsia. Seeing Jon's blank look, he explained, "Pre-eclampsia only happens in pregnant women. For some reason, Gabby's blood pressure is a little high, and she has some swelling in her face, hands and feet. I've placed her on strict bed rest to see if we can get her blood pressure to come down some. I will also give her some medication to help the blood pressure. She is only allowed out of bed to go to the rest room for at least the next two weeks. I wish we had the ability to run some tests, but we don't. Luckily, though, I think we caught it very early." James looked very serious for a moment. "I do need to warn you both that if we can't keep your blood pressure down, we may have to do a C-section a little earlier than your due date to keep the baby from having problems from the elevated blood pressure. I'll be in to check on you frequently, as will Maureen. You can read or sew or sleep- but you need to be lying down, preferably on your left side to keep the weight of the baby off of your major blood vessels. I'll also be talking to Janet about a special diet for you."

Jon and Gabby agreed to everything James told them, but they both looked shell-shocked. Gabby's eyes were welling up with tears. "But how can I help with things if I am lying in bed all day? I want to pull my weight around here, and I can't do that from here."

I held her other hand and told her, "Gabby, dear, you have been working so hard. Right now, the best thing you can do is take good care of my wonderful daughter-in-law and my granddaughter," I said.

"Granddaughter, Mom?" asked Jon. "Do you know something we don't know?"

"Nope – just grandmother's instinct that it is going to be a girl. Now do everything the doctor says. I don't want my granddaughter popping out of the oven half-baked like her father" I said, laughing. Jon rolled his eyes at me, and I reminded him that he and his brother were born early by C-section because of pre-eclampsia, so I knew what I was talking about. The rest of us left the room to give Jon and Gabby some time alone.

We spent the rest of the day checking out equipment to see what survived the EMP. The radios that the security team were using were toast, but all of the equipment Father Dan locked in his cabinets seemed to be functional. Kiara finished hooking up the rest of the solar, and that, too seemed to be working well. The Nuk-Alerts remained quiet all day, and the wind kept up from the west. That was very reassuring.

Late in the afternoon after we finished checking everything, Kiara, Marcie, and I each got a glass of tea and sat out on the steps of the front porch. We were hot and tired, but happy to find out we actually lost very little from the EMP. As we sat there resting, we suddenly heard loud voices coming from the area outside the apartments. It sounded like several people fighting, and we quickly got to our feet and headed over to see what was going on. As we rounded the corner, we were surprised to see Maureen arguing with Anita, one of the dependent wives who lived in the apartments. Several other wives were standing around them, and it seemed that one or two were actually egging Anita on. Both Anita and Maureen were red in the face from yelling at each other.

"What in the world is going on here?" I asked.

Both Maureen and Anita started talking at once. "One at a time," I said. "Maureen, you go first."

"Anita was on the schedule this afternoon to help clean the barn. We waited for her before we started, but she didn't show up, so I came to find her. It's not the first time she's been late, and I thought she might have forgotten. Instead, I found her playing cards and she said she wasn't going to help today." I turned and looked at Anita, who stared back at me with her arms defiantly crossed.

"I am sick and tired of working. Before all this happened, I didn't have to work. I'm an officer's wife. I could go shopping, see a show, visit with friends, and as long as the cleaning lady came twice a week, I had time to do the things I wanted to do. Now, though, every time I turn around, I have to work. I am tired of this. I'm not going to do it and you can't make me. What are you gonna do, dock my pay? It's bad enough we have to live in these crappy apartments with nothing to do, but I don't need this witch hassling me to go pick up cow dung or whatever the heck she wants me to do. I've had it."

"You've had it?" yelled Maureen. "We are out there every single day taking care of the animals, making sure you have milk, eggs, and meat, and you begrudge us a couple of hours of work?" By now, Maureen was in tears, her frustration with Anita getting the better of her. Marcie walked over to Maureen and put her arm around Maureen's shoulders.

"Calm down, my friend. It's not worth getting your blood pressure up like this. Let Denise work it out." Marcie continued to speak quietly to Maureen, and we could see Maureen starting to settle down. I turned back to Anita.

"I can understand that you are tired and stressed out. This situation we've been living in for months has been more than a little bit stressful for all of us. That's not an excuse, though, to shirk your duties." I tried to stay calm and keep my voice level, but it was hard. Anita was defiant, though. She looked at me with a haughty expression and barked, "I am not shirking my duties. I should not have any duties. I didn't come here to work. I came here to be with my husband, who works hard enough for both of us."

I took a deep breath before speaking. "Why do you think you shouldn't have any duties around here? You expect to eat and have clean clothes and a place to sleep, right?"

"You owe that to me because of my husband. He is sacrificing a lot to keep all of you safe. It's bad enough I have to live in the same apartment as enlisted wives. I certainly do not have to continue to do this menial labor you are inflicting on us."

Kiara had remained silent thus far, but she stepped close to Anita and looked down at her, frowning. "Anita, I don't know who you think you are, but I seriously recommend you reconsider what you just said"

"Or what? Are you going to throw me out? My husband won't like that, and he can make it very difficult for you civilians."

Kiara took a deep breath, and I could see her clenching her fists in anger. "First of all, I am not a civilian. I am active duty military and I outrank your husband. Second, you've got some nerve. Denise and her team took you in when you had nowhere to go, and this is how you treat them? You think you are better than others because your husband is a lieutenant? Let me tell you something. Being an officer, or even an officer's wife means you need to work harder than the others. Your job is to be a great example, a mentor to the ranks. Your job is to do your best to help take care of people, be a role model and a supporter, not waltz around here acting like you are the Queen Mother or something." I had never seen Kiara, who was always so happy and upbeat, act so angry. She took a breath and continued speaking.

"You do not deserve to be here, and I pity your husband. Before the collapse, you would just be a liability to him and to his career. Now, though, you are liable to get him killed. You disgust me."

I was making a valiant effort to not lose my temper. I couldn't believe the attitude this woman was displaying. Of course, when she made the crack about the enlisted wives, several of the other women looked offended and stepped back.

Kiara reached over to take Maureen's arm. "Come on, Maureen. Let's go get something cold to drink. You don't need to put up with this." Maureen gave Kiara a grateful look and walked away with her.

I watched Kiara and Maureen walk away for a minute or so, and then turned back to Anita.

"You are living here on my land in my building, eating the food that my friends and I gathered and put up. In exchange for a safe place to live, you are expected to help with chores. You signed yourself up for the barn duties and I expect you to carry out your obligations. If you do not like the rules here, you are welcome to leave."

"And just where do you expect me to go?"

"I don't care. The choice is yours. Either you pitch in and do chores like every other person here, or else you leave."

I could see she was really working herself up into hysteria, so I turned away and pulled out my radio.

"Mark, do you copy?"

"Roger, what's up?"

"I need you and Second Lieutenant Braxton over here at the apartments right away."

"Roger, is someone hurt?"

"Not yet. Just hurry."

Anita turned to walk away, and I stopped her. "You just wait right here until they get here." As Anita tried to step away, the enlisted wives who had stepped away from her before closed in, blocking her way. Anita folded her arms again and gave several dramatic sighs, rolling her eyes, but nobody moved out of her way. We stood like that for a few minutes. Finally, we could hear an ATV roaring towards us. Mark and 2LT Braxton jumped off the ATV and hurried towards us.

"What's going on, Denise? Is everything okay?" Mark asked.

"Actually, everything is not okay. This young lady seems to think she is too good to help with chores and is refusing to help. She believes that because she is an officer's wife, she is above what she calls menial labor." I could see 2LT Braxton's expression go from concerned to confused to upset. Ignoring everyone else, he walked up to Anita and took her arm.

"Nita, what is wrong with you? You know we all have to work if we are going to survive. How could you be this way?"

"Oh, Pete, when we got married, you promised me I wouldn't have to work if I didn't want to. Look at my hands, all chapped and my nails chipped from working like a common servant. I'm tired of it. Tell these people you promised me I didn't have to work."

"Anita, that was before the world ended. Now we all have to do everything we can to survive. That means there is no such thing anymore as not having to work. If you don't work, you don't eat."

"So now you are threatening me, too? I don't know why I married you if you are going to tell me lies and not take care of me. Go away. Leave me alone. I don't want to see any of you anymore. I am going to pack my bags and head back home to our house in Spring Lake. The heck with all of you."

Pete Braxton looked at his wife with a sorrowful expression on his face. "Our house is almost certainly gone after that nuke last night. You have nowhere to go but here. We are incredibly lucky to be here and together. Even if it means we have to work hard, at least we are alive and relatively safe."

While the lieutenant was talking with his wife, I saw James approaching with something in his hand. When he got close enough, he addressed Anita in a soft, calming voice.

"Anita, I can see you are pretty upset. I have some medication with me to help you calm down and rest. Will you let me give you some medication to help you?" Anita looked at her husband, who nodded yes.

"All right. Yes, I need something to help me." James asked Pete to accompany his wife to their apartment to administer the injection in private. After he gave the shot, he instructed Pete to stay with Anita until she fell asleep. He explained that the sedative would probably help her sleep for a few hours.

When James came back outside, he walked over to Mark and me. "She is having a mental break, probably as a result of everything she's been through. I will talk to Father Dan and see if we can set up some counseling for her. I am also going to start her on some antidepressants to help her cope a little better. We need to be supportive of her if we want her to get better. Let's take her off chores for a couple of days until the medication starts to work."

I was glad James was able to do something to help her, but I was concerned that others would start having issues as well. When I voiced this to James, he said he fully expected a couple of people would not be able to stand the pressure, and we just needed to keep our eyes open for others who seemed to be struggling. I thanked James and asked him how he knew to come over with the medication.

"Well, it's not like I couldn't hear all the yelling, but Kiara and Maureen came to find me to tell me they thought Anita was in need of medical intervention and explained what was going on."

I thanked James and Mark and told them I was headed back to the house. Just what we needed was something else to worry about. How many more folks on the farm would start having mental issues from all of the stress? When I got back to the house, I shut myself up in my office with a psychology textbook. I was still reading when Tom came to get me for supper.

"I think I need to talk to Father Dan about setting up some sessions for folks who are starting to feel the stress of all that is going on," I told him as soon as he walked in.

Tom looked at me with a frown. "Are you one of those people?" he asked.

"I could be with everything I'm worried about right now, but I think I am still coping okay. After the big battle this afternoon, though, I am worried about some of the others."

"What big battle? What did I miss?"

"The big battle between Maureen and one of the wives. They were both yelling at each other, and apparently the woman just lost it. James had to medicate her to settle down and I still don't know what we will do with her once her mood is a bit more settled."

"Are you thinking of kicking her out?"

"Tom, you don't know how much I'd like to, but I can't. I don't think she can really help her behavior, but I think she can help her attitude. I'm willing to give her a chance if she will do the work that she is scheduled to do. If she refuses to work, though, she is going to have to go somewhere else – but where can she go? It is such a quandary."

"Well, what about sending her to the new housing development. Maybe if she is working on a home for her and her husband, it will help her cope a little better."

"That is a great idea. I'll talk to Mark about it in the morning. Thank you. You always seem to have good ideas and suggestions for me."

"Okay, then, how about this for an idea. I suggest we go eat dinner." I laughed, and we strolled over to the dining hall, arm in arm.

After dinner, we had a community meeting to talk about our new project with Mark. The meeting was short because while everyone had a lot of ideas and seemed enthusiastic, we really did not know what we had to work with. We decided to wait to make any plans until Tom and I could see the community and get some ideas of what was needed. After about twenty minutes of talking, we adjourned our meeting and even though it was still early, I headed off to bed.

CHAPTER FOUR

The next morning, Tom and I geared up and went to meet Mark at the barracks. Mark was accompanied by a group of soldiers and two MRAPs were parked nearby. I noticed one of the MRAPs was towing a large trailer. Mark called us all together to explain our plan for the day.

"We are going to drive through the community to the elementary school. It's located pretty much in the middle of the subdivision. We've been through the subdivision a number of times and have never seen anyone. I really figured if people were not in their homes, they may have moved into the school. The last time we were here, though, there wasn't anyone in the school. My plan is to check the school again to be sure it is vacant. We are leaving six of the soldiers here to essentially guard the school. The trailer holds the supplies they will need, as well as some other things that we thought would be useful. We'll use the school as our base of operations as we work on this community. Today, we'll focus on updating the map to show what houses are here, which ones have been destroyed, and if we see any that look occupied. After we do that, our next task will be to give the school a good cleaning so that if we do have citizens come volunteer to work with us to rebuild, we have a clean and safe place for them to stay until homes are ready to be occupied. I've got a large map of this area, and we brought a couple of drones to help us, so we don't have to walk so far to map everything out."

I looked at Mark with a puzzled expression on my face. "I thought you didn't have any drones? At least, that's what Carter said."

Mark grinned. "We didn't, but General McPherson does, and he gave us a couple. In addition to marking homes, garages, and outbuildings, I want to mark any areas that would be useful as community gardens or places where we could stable animals. I think there are two churches in the subdivision, but I don't know what condition they are in. After we do an overview with the drones, we will then drive street to street to get a better look at what we have to work with. Any questions?" He looked around and nobody seemed to have any questions, so he told us to load up and we headed into town.

Although I had been to town numerous times since the collapse on scavenging trips, it still was painful to see the damage and destruction that had occurred. I was glad that we were going to be reversing some of that damage. After driving through miles of burned out shells of buildings, we finally arrived at the Whispering Willows subdivision. I was happy to see the gates to the community were closed and locked. Mark explained that his troops fixed the gate last time they were there and added the chain and lock to keep the area secure. One of the soldiers hopped out of the other MRAP and unlocked the gate.

After we drove through, he locked the gate back up, and we continued driving. The homes within looked to be in better condition than many of the homes in Riverdale, although there was still obvious evidence of looting, and there were a few homes destroyed by fire. Most of the homes that burned were near the outer fence. It made me wonder if people who were not able to get over the fence just burned the nearest homes out of spite. The homes in this development were a bit larger than most of the homes in Riverdale, and the lots seemed to be a little larger. Grass had grown up quite a bit since last fall, and some of the homes looked like they had overgrown and untended gardens. I made a mental note to check these gardens to see if there were any "volunteer" plants that came back on their own from last year's crop.

We soon arrived at the elementary school. There were no signs of life around the school. The grass and shrubs were overgrown, and there were several broken windows that we could see. The deserted playground struck me as so sad, watching a lone swing moving with the breeze. I hoped that before long, the playground would again be alive with the sound of happy children. Mark called me back from my playground daydreams and told us to stay in the MRAP until he and his men were sure the school was safe. It only took them about 15 minutes, and then Mark was back. He reached into the MRAP and pulled out a large briefcase before inviting us in. As we entered, two of his soldiers were headed to the front door to keep watch.

I was quite surprised that the inside of the school did not seem to have been disturbed. Everything was very dusty, and there was some trash and debris littering the floor, but other than that, it looked like school had just let out. There was artwork on the walls, and the parent's sign-out book was still sitting on the counter at the main office. We walked further to the cafeteria. It was surprisingly bright due to large windows near the ceiling and several skylights.

Mark looked around and said, "I think this is where we will set up. We've got plenty of table space, and we can use the bulletin boards to post our maps." He directed several of his troops to move a few tables together near the bulletin boards and asked me if I could try to find a broom so we could clear an area to start working. Tom and I went out of the cafeteria and found a janitor's closet down one of the hallways. Instead of just the broom, I grabbed the entire cleaning cart, along with a couple of bottles of cleaner and a bag of rags on one of the shelves.

We pushed the cart back to the cafeteria, where the men had already moved tables and Mark was tacking maps up onto the bulletin board. I grabbed the cleaner and a couple of rags and started wiping down the tables and chairs while Tom and one of the soldiers took the two brooms and started sweeping. It only took about 40 minutes to make the room a lot cleaner. Of course, it needed more than a quick wipe-down, but at least the majority of the dust and trash was gone.

While we were finishing up the cleaning effort, Mark set up two of his men with the drones. Each man had a small tablet contraption that controlled the drones and sent back pictures from the cameras mounted on each drone. Mark also had two laptops set up on the table nearest the maps with one soldier at each lap top. Tom and I must have looked a bit perplexed because Mark then explained that each laptop was set up to also see the pictures from the drones, so the men could mark their observations onto the maps. He finished giving instructions to the men with the drones, and they left to go launch their drones. He walked over to another table away from the maps and lap tops and invited us to sit down.

"While the guys are doing preliminary surveillance, I wanted to talk with you both about how we are going to put this effort together. My men and I know how to swing a hammer, but this project is going to take a lot more than just you telling us what to nail together. Tom, you are an awesome contractor, as you proved over and over with all the construction we did at the farm, so I want you to oversee the actual construction efforts here. Denise, you are one of the most organized people I've ever met, so I am hoping you will have some ideas on the big picture."

"Wow, Mark, you are going to make my head swell. I do have some ideas, though. Let me think this through out loud." I noticed Mark pulled out a notepad and prepared to take notes. "Have you ever heard of Habitat for Humanity?" Both men shook their heads no. "This is an excellent organization that builds homes for people who otherwise could not afford it. The thing is, though, the new homeowners have to invest sweat equity in the home. They need to help in whatever capacity they can to build the house. I really like that idea because it is not a give-away program. Homeowners earn their home, and it helps them be more engaged and invested than if they were just handed the keys without any effort on their part. I think whatever we do, we need to avoid giveaways. People are going to be very needy, but we don't need to strip them of their dignity and independence by providing everything. After all, we really need them to be as self-sufficient as possible. We'll need to think of how we can set that up."

"That is a great idea," Mark interjected. "We could set up some kind of barter – they need a home, and these are the things they need to do to get one. Same for food, clothes, and other things."

"Exactly! Get them in the habit from the beginning that we all work together and nothing comes for free." I was happy that Mark understood what I meant.

"I have a few ideas about the actual work getting this place ready. First, we need to identify which homes are salvageable. Homes that are not salvageable can still be used for raw materials and anything inside that might have survived. I would suggest that we take down the unusable homes, as that will give more land to farm or to house animals. That will also give us more raw materials to use in homes we can fix. We will need to designate a place to store the things we remove from the homes we tear down. Construction materials can go outside, but things like dishes, clothes, and furniture will need to be stored out of the weather. It might be a good idea to use a few classrooms and designate one for kitchen supplies, one for linens and household equipment, one for food and pantry supplies we may find, and so on. That way, we can sort things as we put them away and it will make it easier to find them later on. We'll also need to store things we find in the homes that may be special to the family like pictures and stuff. We can store them in boxes and if the family comes back, their special things will still be there." I stopped for a minute to think and Mark kept writing.

"We'll need to identify who the owners of each home are, so that if those people come back, they can have their own home back. We will also need to develop a registry of people who do move back here to know what kind of skills they have and also what kind of needs they have.

"We'll need to think about setting up a medical clinic, because unless people were really prepared like we were, I think we will probably see a lot of poor health at first. We will probably also need to set up a community kitchen to begin with. Mark, has anyone checked the kitchen here in the school?"

Mark's eyes got big. "No, other than making sure there was no-one back there, we didn't really look." He called over to one of the soldiers who was just watching the drone footage and had him go look to see what he could find in the kitchen.

"We'll need to get a crew together to clean this building first. But, in order to clean, it would be nice to have power and water. Power we can get from a generator or solar, but we need to figure out water.

"I think we should empty out the houses we repair and put everything into the classrooms. When we move a family in, they can come get the supplies they need. That way, things won't go to waste as much as if we left everything in the houses whether or not the family needed it.

"We need to get a group of us to go door to door checking to see if people are there, and to leave some kind of flyer or brochure telling them how to register with us so we know not to touch their house. We also need to start scavenging local unoccupied farms to see if there are cattle, horses, or other animals running loose that we can bring here. If that doesn't work, we will have to try some of the local farms that are still in operation to see if anyone is willing to part with some. I know we can surely spare a couple of pigs, chickens, and rabbits to get them started.

"We also need to look at any building that is not a home – for example, the little strip mall across the street looks like it has been gone through, but we need to look closely to see if there are things that were missed.

"There is a big field out behind the school. We need to get Andrew or some of your farm-boy soldiers over here with a tractor to see if we can get a garden put in, sooner rather than later. I'm sure we have enough seeds to spare to get these people started." I stopped to think for a minute. "I am sure there is more, but that's what I have for now. We need to prioritize all of this, though, because we can't do it all at once."

Mark and Tom both chuckled. "Gee, I thought you'd have it all done by this afternoon." Mark said. "Let's take a walk through the school and identify what rooms we are going to use for storage and what rooms can be used to house people to begin with." We started walking through the school. The halls were full of artwork done by the children, and as we walked past, I wondered about the children that drew each picture. Were they safe? Did they have enough to eat? I could feel my eyes welling up, and so I shook my head and kept walking. Thinking about that could drive me crazy, and I needed to focus on what we could do to help. I stopped as we passed the principal's office. "Mark, this would make a good place for you to set up shop as the overall leadership of the community." I turned the knob, expecting the door to be locked, but to my surprise, it opened. We walked into a spacious anteroom with several desks. One desk had a microphone and a panel for contacting each classroom, obviously non-functional without power. There were three doors in the anteroom. I opened one and found a large walk-in supply closet. There were shelves full of pencils, paper, crayons, and other school supplies. Several shelves were completely empty, and I assumed they once held some type of food or other useful items. The next door led to a rest room. I opened the third door and entered the principal's private office. It was a very functional office with a desk in the middle, several large file cabinets taking up one wall, and a smaller file cabinet in the corner behind the desk. There were several stacks of paper on the desk, so I went behind the desk and sat down. Picking up the first stack, I saw it was a list of children with addresses and parent's names. Many names on the list were lined through. A few names were circled, and there were other names with question marks. Next to the lined-out names were numbers. I asked Tom and Mark if they had any idea what these numbers meant.

Tom took the list from me and started reading. "I wonder if this list is of students who the principal knew left or who were safe? But what is with the numbers after some of the names?" He paused, and suddenly, his head shot up. "There is one thing that I would expect to see at a school when the school is closed – school buses. But, I didn't see a single one. The parking lot for the buses is empty. Look, some of the numbers are repeated several times. I wonder if they loaded the kids up and took them somewhere, and these numbers are either the bus number or else the location of where the kids went." Mark and I both nodded agreement.

"You are brilliant" I said. "At least, you are if that's what the numbers mean!" I grinned at Tom, and then continued. "But look, there is an address for each child on the list. We could add that to the map and know who the owners were of each home." I stood up and walked over to the smaller file cabinet. "I am betting in one of the file cabinets, we will find a folder for each child that lists age, siblings, parents' names and other helpful information. I wonder if the general might have a couple of clerks with laptops who could come gather all that data into one file? That would certainly help resettling people."

Mark nodded. "Yes, I am sure we can get the general to send us a couple of his clerks to help out."

I looked at the list in my hand. "I wonder what the circles and question marks mean? There is no number so maybe it means the principal did not know about some people or they chose to stay here." I started opening file drawers, and Tom and Mark did the same to the other file cabinets in the room.

"Bingo!" exclaimed Mark. "Here we go, folders labeled 'current students'. I'll call the general and see about those clerks. Meanwhile, let's continue looking at rooms." We left the office and headed down the halls. We must have been in the upper grade hallway, because the rooms looked like they were set up for older kids. We identified a number of rooms as storage and picked out several of the larger ones to house temporary residents. We put handwritten signs on each door indicating the planned use of each room. We then started down the next hallway. This was obviously kindergarten territory. The rooms were large with a lot of windows. Each room had a stack of mats for nap time, and there were areas set aside for reading, blocks, and other activities. I commented that this area would make a great place for a day care area while we are building. Watching kids while parents were working could be one way to work in exchange for supplies and stuff.

When we had been down all four hallways, we returned to the cafeteria. The soldier we sent to check the kitchen was waiting for us with a list of all the items he found. Mark took the list, thanked the soldier, and quickly skimmed through to see what he found. "We're in luck. It seems that whoever cleaned out the majority of the food in the kitchen left some big things behind. It looks like he found some large tubs of large tubs of flour, rice, and sugar. He also found several large jugs of cooking oil, several large cans of vegetables, a big can of salt, two jars of yeast, a case of individual ketchup packets, and three cases of bottled water. I suppose these were things that were missed when they cleaned out the food from the kitchen or else they ran out of room. There are also industrial sized pots and pans, and a gas stove and fryer. Not a lot of stuff, but more than we had when we got here."

Mark walked over to where the troops were watching the drone video and marking the maps. "Hey, Gibson, are you guys almost done?"

Sergeant Gibson looked up, and answered, "Yes, sir. They are bringing the drones in now. We just finished marking the maps with what we saw." Tom and I crowded in next to Mark to look at the maps. There were more homes destroyed than I anticipated, and a lot of smaller outbuildings marked. The two churches were also shown. The one on the far side of the development looked like it had burned, but the other looked to be in pretty good condition. Mark asked if we were ready to go driving and called one of the soldiers over to accompany us. Private Cooper barely looked old enough to be in the army and seemed excited to be selected for the ride.

As we headed out to the MRAP I realized I still had the list of children in my hand. I suggested we ought to check the houses that were either circled or had a question mark to see if there was anyone there. The guys thought that was a good idea and so we headed out. As we came to a street, Tom would call out the name of the street, and I would search the list for a circle or a question mark. The first home on the list was a question mark. We pulled into the driveway and noticed there was a lot of damage to the home, including broken windows and the front door hanging open. As we looked closer, we could see bullet holes in the front walls of the house. We waited a few minutes to see if we saw any movement from the house. After about five minutes, Mark and Private Cooper got out of the MRAP and approached the house. They carefully cleared the area around the house, and then went in. Ten long minutes later, both exited the house. The younger soldier looked very pale. Mark just looked angry as they both got back into the MRAP.

"The house is probably salvageable, but we will need a burial detail before we can work here. The family must have been attacked by raiders of some sort. There are two adults and three children in the master bedroom, and all were shot execution style." Mark balled his fists up and took a deep breath.

"The youngest child didn't look much older than a toddler. We still don't know if the question mark means the principal didn't know or if the students are dead. Let's check out the next one." The next student on the list was circled and was four houses down from the first one. As we pulled into the driveway, we could see that this home was far worse than the first, also with bullet holes across the front wall of the house.

All of the windows seemed to be broken, and tattered curtains fluttered out of one of the upstairs window openings. Mark and Private Cooper again approached the house and carefully entered. This time, they were back out in less than five minutes. Private Cooper rushed to the side of the house where he bent over and vomited. When finished, he stood, rinsed his mouth with water from his canteen, and wiped his mouth with a bandanna. He began to apologize, but Mark stopped him. Getting into the MRAP, Mark explained to us that the family here was also dead, but rather than being executed, this family was tortured first. "I'm not going to describe it to you because I don't want you having that picture in your head. It was terrible."

Private Cooper looked like he was about to cry. "How could they do things like that to women and especially to little kids like that?" Mark reached over and put a hand on his shoulder.

"Son, there are all kinds of animals in the world who took this collapse to mean they could do all of the evil, perverted things they could only dream about before. If we catch people who did things like that, we can make sure they suffer just like that family did." Our ride was silent as we found houses matching circled names on the list. Each of these had the same results – bodies of families found dead. We concluded that circled homes meant the family was dead, and question marks meant the principal just did not know. We checked a few of the homes with question marks, and a couple still held the bodies of families, but most were empty. Several had evidence the family left, and one even had a note on the kitchen table indicating they left to go to "Grampa's farm." I hope they made it there safely.

We had a pleasant surprise at the first church we came to. Several men, all armed, were out in the back of the church working on a garden. Mark and PVT Cooper carefully approached them, only to learn there were five families living in the church basement. Once everyone decided we were all friendly, the men called others out of the church. Several ladies and a handful of kids came out to meet us. We quickly explained what we were doing, and all of the families seemed very excited. They explained they heard gunshots on the far side of the community and decided to hide in the church.

They gathered as much food and supplies as they could and moved into the basement. Luckily, the church had a food bank, and so they had enough food to get through the winter. Now that it was getting on to spring, they decided to plant a garden to supplement what was left. While the men were talking, I spoke with the ladies. Everyone seemed really healthy, and one of the women attributed that to vitamins and making sure they ate regularly.

During the winter, the men shot two deer, and that gave them enough meat for everyone for the winter. They said they had a lot of rice and beans to eat, but it beat the alternative of starving. I asked if kids used to go to the local elementary school, and three of the moms said they did. I found their names on my list with a question mark after each one, and happily crossed out the question marks.

All five families indicated they would like to be able to move back to their homes, but not until they made repairs and they felt the neighborhood was safe. They also said they would be willing to move to other homes closer to the school if they could get personal things from their homes, which were farther away from the school. I asked about the minister for the church and was told that he died over the winter of what they think was pneumonia and heart failure and was buried in the prayer garden on the other side of the church.

We stayed to chat for about a half an hour, until Tom remarked it was getting late and we needed to get back. The four of us said goodbye to our new friends with promises to be back soon and headed back to the school. We dropped Private Cooper off at the school, as he was one of the soldiers who would be staying. Mark went in to get the soldiers coming back with us but came out by himself. He explained the guys wanted to put the drones up in the dark to see if they could see light in any of the houses. I thought that was a pretty good idea.

We sat in the MRAP for a few minutes going over the lists of tasks Mark had assembled over the day, and then headed for the farm.

The ride back was fairly quiet. Mark was obviously preoccupied with something, and Tom and I were just tired. Finally, I asked Mark if he was okay since he was so quiet. I could see him clenching his jaws as he considered what to say.

"I've been in the military for a long time. I've been a lot of places and seen a lot of things that I would not ever want to see again. That one house, though, the torture that was inflicted on that young family, well, it was beyond anything I've ever seen before. If I could catch the scum who did that…" His voice faded off. "Unfortunately, I suspect it will not be the last time we see evidence of how evil some people can be. It motivates me, though, to try to get this development up and running and do what we can to help people. I mean, people did not ask for all of this to happen. I want to be able to help the good people out there, and to protect them from the monsters who would hurt them."

We got back to the farm right before dinner. After a quick meal, we called everyone together to give them the details of our trip. We skimmed lightly over the bodies we found, although most people could tell there was more than we were willing to say.

"On the ride home, Tom, Mark, and I went over the long list of things to be done and we established some priorities. The first priority will be to get the school cleaned up, inside and out. We plan to use the school as the headquarters for this operation. We'll use some of the rooms for storage, some for a day care area, and some to house people who are working on their homes until the homes are ready. We'll also have an area for the soldiers who are providing security until we can find a proper home for them, too.

"The outside of the school will also need some work, as the grass has gotten pretty high over the last few months. There is a big field next to the school where we want to put a community garden. Andrew, I know you are really busy here with all of our fields, but I was hoping you could give a couple of soldiers some direction in what needs to be done to get it ready for a garden.

"Once the school is done, we will start on the homes on the same block as the school. We've already met some folks living in the development who are willing to help fix these homes and move into them. As we get a block fixed and people moved in, we'll move to the next block, and so on, working around the school.

"There are also some small stores across from the school. The goal is to get them cleaned up also and use them as places to start businesses – places where the community can barter, maybe a medical clinic, and so on. That is farther down the list though. First, we need to get homes repaired and people moved in."

Tom then talked about his observations of the type of work that would need to be done. "From a construction point of view, there are a number of houses that need repairs to doors and windows. Quite a few have bullet holes that will need to be repaired. I noticed the winter was not kind to many of the roofs which are missing shingles. There are a few homes that are beyond repair. Some are burned, and some are just in bad shape. We will take those homes apart as best we can and salvage any materials we can to use in houses that can be repaired."

Marcie raised her hand and asked, "What about all of the stuff inside each house? What will you do with things like dishes and furniture?"

"Good question," I responded. We plan to empty each house before it is repaired. We will then clean the items removed and store them in designated areas in the school. We'll use them to supply families as they move into newly repaired homes. Stuff that is badly damaged will just be discarded, I suppose."

"What about people who return to the community and want to stay in their own home?" asked Janet.

"We'll help them fix their home if they want, and of course, they can stay there. We are not about to take away people's homes, although our first five families are willing to move to homes closer to the school for safety," answered Tom.

We spent another half hour talking over all of the work that would be involved and decided we would have a small group of us go to the school in a few days to begin cleaning. Talk then turned to the EMP and to the bombing of Fort Bragg. The Nuk-Alerts remained silent, which was encouraging to know there was either no radiation involved, or the wind continued to blow it all away from us. Tom and I assured everyone that we did not have any additional information about Fort Bragg but would share anything we may learn.

I was thrilled to learn the solar was working as well as it was before the EMP. Everyone applauded Kiara for the great job she did getting everything hooked up and working again. Father Dan reported the radios and computers all survived the EMP. We only lost the radio Tom was holding and two of the radios held by our security folks. Janet reported the kitchen equipment was again working fine, and nothing was lost. All in all, we were extraordinarily lucky.

When our meeting was over, I headed over to Jon's wing of the house to check on Gabby. I found her resting in bed with her sister-in-law Stacy and nephew John Henry at her side.

"How are you feeling?" I asked.

"Better, I think. My blood pressure is down a bit and my headache has eased up a little bit. I feel really guilty just laying around, but Stacy has been keeping me company. Plus, I've been enjoying playing with the baby."

Stacy chimed in, "Yes, and I keep reminding her that she needs to stay in bed and rest if she wants to be able to play with her own baby one of these days."

I reached over and picked up my grandson. He was almost six months old and was a happy baby. As I tickled him under his chin, he grinned widely and reminded me so much of his daddy at the same age. I played with him for a while, making all kinds of silly sounds just to hear him giggle. Playing with him was about the best stress relief I could find.

Later that night, as I tried to go to sleep, I tried to picture what kind of world my grandchildren would inherit. I hoped we were successful on the small scale in Riverdale, but also on the large scale. I wanted my grandkids to know all of the freedoms I had growing up. That meant we really needed to work hard now to have something for them later on. As I was falling asleep, my last thought was that I forgot to talk to Mark about Anita.

CHAPTER FIVE

At precisely 1400, General McPherson drove into the main entrance of the airport. He was quite pleased to see that his troops had already moved some of the non-functional airplanes out of hangers to make room for their tanks and missile systems. The fence around the airport had been reinforced with additional barbed wire, and there was now a guard station at the main gate.

The adjoining college campus was also partially fenced off so that the dormitories and several classroom buildings were now part of the airport complex. As he approached the main terminal, General McPherson noted the hand-painted sign that read "United States Army Special Operations Command (Airborne) (USASOC)." Sammy was standing next to the sign waiting to greet the general. As General McPherson stepped out of his Humvee and returned Sammy's salute, he pointed to the sign and grinned. "That's a nice touch, General."

"Thank you, sir. It's all about the optics, you know." The general and Sammy both laughed.

"How much trouble did you have occupying the area?"

"Not much, Mac. There were a couple of young people living in one part of one of the dorms. We helped them move to one of the classrooms outside the fence, brought them some additional furniture and things that they needed, and promised to help them get water going once we were settled in. They were grateful for the help and acted very happy to see us. Nice kids, they were going to college here when things fell apart and had nowhere else to go, no way to get home, so they stayed here."

"No problems with the airport?"

"No, sir, the airport was completely vacant. It was pretty creepy, and I had a few of the guys go through looking for any kind of booby traps. They didn't find any traps, but we did find a lot of av gas, as well as a couple of large tanks of diesel. We also checked out the air traffic control tower. Naturally, with no power, none of the systems there are working, but I know where I can find an electrical engineer who might be able to get some of this running again if we can get power going. First Lieutenant Kiara Diamond was one of the troops Mark evacuated from Bragg on their way here, and he tells me she is brilliant when it comes to anything electronic."

"Well, get her out here then, because we need to have radar up as soon as possible. Have the big generators that we had hidden in the caves arrived yet?"

"Yes, they are in the first hangar. We did not want them out in the open, since we've not yet found the sleeper cell we suspect is here. When 1LT Diamond gets here, we'll have her check them all out before we fire them up. We've set up the terminal area to be our main conference area, with some private space for you. We also have an area set up here for us to be billeted here. I didn't think you wanted to be all the way over by the dorms, as that's where we're putting most of the troops." General McPherson was grinning widely.

"Well done. I can tell you must have been working all night, and you did a good job. Show me where our conference area is so that we can get busy."

Sammy escorted the general to a large room with a table and chairs in the middle and several smaller tables along the sides. One corner of the room was set up to be a communications center with several radios and two radio operators.

"The big table is for meetings with your commanders. The tables around the sides are where various people will work. There are several smaller rooms off to your left set up as both offices and sleeping quarters. There is also a small room where you can have private meetings." Sammy escorted the general on a tour of the small rooms. "I hope you don't mind, but I went ahead and had your stuff moved into your quarters."

"You did a great job, Sammy. I'm assuming this is my office?" said the general, pointing to a small room next to his quarters.

"Yes, sir. I'll be in the office next to you, and Carter can take the one just past my office."

"Excellent. I am going to go get settled in my office and try to get some work done. In about an hour or so, let's take a tour of the airport and campus so you can show me the lay of the land. Meanwhile, do we have a coffee pot anywhere around here?"

Sammy just laughed. "There is one out in the big room next to the radios. Do you want me to get you a cup?"

"Have you ever known me to turn down a cup of coffee? Make it a big cup... oh, and Sammy? Thank you." Sammy grinned as he left, shutting the office door behind him.

General McPherson sat at his new desk and opened his worn briefcase. He pulled out a stack of reports he received that morning from the various unit commanders with him in Riverdale. He looked at the first report, which was a headcount of all the people currently on their new base. As he skimmed through the list, he was reassured to see that not only did he have a large number of combat-ready troops, he also had a good number of soldiers with critical skills including medical, engineering, communications, and support staff. The second report listed all of the equipment they had from Fort Bragg. He was surprised at how long the list was: the unit commanders did a great job of moving a lot of heavy equipment, combat vehicles, and armament from Bragg to the caves.

The next report addressed current stocks of weapons and ammunition. While it was a good amount, he knew that you could never have too many guns or too much ammunition. He looked quickly through the list to see if the armorers with him had the materials necessary to reload ammunition. When he didn't see that information after a quick skim, he pulled a yellow lined note pad from his briefcase and started a list. In addition to ammunition, he added medical staff and supplies to the list. Just then, Sammy returned with a pot of coffee and two mugs.

"I'm sorry it took so long," Sammy said. "I had to make fresh and it took a few minutes to find potable water to use."

"No problem," the general replied. "I've been skimming through these reports and trying to establish some priorities for us on this base before we start tackling Homeland troops. At the top of the list is food and water. We need to get a large garden in. I wonder if those young people you moved into a classroom would be willing to help with a garden in exchange for food and water? That would free up troops for other tasks."

Sammy looked thoughtful for a moment. "I know that when I talked with them, they seemed to be interested in helping us any way they could. I'll send someone over later to have a chat with them."

"Good. Let me know what they say. The next thing on the list is getting a medical aid station set up. I see we have a few medical staff with us, and we'll probably need to look for medical supplies."

Sammy smiled. "I've got the answers on that one. The medical folks have already taken over a section of the ground floor of one of the dorms and they are setting up a medical area. I'll find out what kind of medical staff they have. They seem to have quite a lot of equipment and supplies, but I'll have them make a wish list for scavenging."

"Good. I'm glad they took the initiative to find an area and get set up. Next, we will need to find our armorers. I didn't see reloading equipment listed, but I was just skimming pretty quickly. We need to be sure that all troops understand to save their brass whenever possible, as I am sure there will come a time that ammo is in short supply." Sammy nodded his agreement.

"I want to see all field grade officers here at 2000 tonight so we can start hammering out some plans. We've got a lot of work to do, and I don't think Homeland is going to give us a lot of time to get it all done."

"I'll get the word out to everyone. We should have a much better idea of what we have and what we need by then."

"Thanks, Sammy. Hey, make sure coffee is on the scavenging lists, OK?" Sammy shook his head, laughing as he went out the door.

"I'll be back in an hour to take you on the royal tour. If you need anything before I get back, Sergeant Weaver and Corporal Alvarez are on the radios."

General McPherson gave a distracted wave from behind his desk as he dove back into his paperwork.

An hour later, the two generals took a quick tour of the new base. General McPherson was really impressed with how fast his troops had worked to organize their new base. The airport had six hangers. Three were large commercial hangers, and these had been emptied of planes and most of their combat vehicles and equipment were now stored in them. The other three hangers were smaller, designed to house private planes. These planes were also removed from the hangers, and each hanger was set up as a place for troops to sleep. One hanger had a sign out front that said "Reception." General McPherson headed into that hanger and found rows of cots neatly set up. Off to the side of the room were racks holding sheets and blankets. Other racks held boxes of toiletries and items of clothing. A small crew was busy organizing paperwork at several long tables near the entrance. When they saw the two generals, they immediately came to attention. Sammy smiled at them, put them at ease, and asked them to explain to General McPherson what they were doing. The young lieutenant in charge of the squad stepped forward.

"We're preparing for new arrivals, sir. Some will be displaced military who will need to be processed and placed into units here. Others will be military family members and civilians. They will also need to be processed, and then placed in housing. Right now, we don't have housing set up, but we understand there is a community not far from here that is being fixed up for any non-military personnel. As each person comes in, we will interview them and collect demographic information. We'll assign them to a temporary bed and give them blankets and, if they need it, toiletries and clothing. We have a room set up behind us that will be staffed with medics who will give each person a quick health check – we don't want to have lice or other infectious things in here. Once released by the medics, people will go through a brief orientation, and then will wait here until they have either a military assignment, or a housing assignment. If they don't pass the medic's exam, they will be sent over to the medical area for treatment before being processed."

General McPherson nodded, expressed his appreciation for their good work, and he and Sammy continued their tour. Both men were encouraged to see the progress that had been made, and that everyone they saw seemed to be in good spirits. After completing their tour, the generals headed back to their offices to begin preparing for the meeting that night.

A few minutes before 2000, the conference area was filled with officers awaiting the general. The room was buzzing with speculation about what would be shared. Most of the men and women in the room were exhausted by all of the work that had been accomplished moving to the new base and getting things set up in a very short time, but they still seemed to have positive attitudes. At 2000, the general entered the room. The officers snapped to attention, and the general quickly put them at ease and had them take their seats. He took a moment to look at the faces of his senior officers and felt a wave of affection for them all.

"Ladies and gentlemen, thank you for coming to this meeting tonight. I know you are all probably pretty tired from all of the excellent work that was done this afternoon. I am very impressed with the progress that was made in one day. Because I know you all need some rack time, I will try to keep this meeting short. I just got off the radio with Admiral Hoskins from the Joint Chiefs to let him know our status. He told me that the Homeland forces seem to be massing in the Alexandria area again. They are using bait and bleed techniques to try to wear down the troops there, but so far, our side is not falling for the bait. Losses on our side have been fairly minimal, but we are concerned that as they mass, they may try to overwhelm our forces. Carter, can you give us information on your units up there?"

Carter stood, a sheaf of papers in his hand. "Yes sir. I currently have four companies of Rangers spread out over the area. They are working with the local militias which consist of about four thousand citizens. I have two additional special forces units that are headed to the area. The Joint Chiefs have directed several battalions from both the 82nd and 101st to be ready to jump in if it looks like the enemy is getting ready to attempt any kind of surge tactics." Carter stood for a moment, looking around in case there were questions. When there were none, he sat back down and the general continued his briefing.

"Thank you. Right now, the UN troops are still not engaging in any combat operations, although they are reported to be harassing the civilian population, taking guns, food, and any other supplies people may have. This is at the direction of Homeland. Apparently, they are trying to remove the ability of citizens to take care of themselves so they are completely dependent on Homeland for food, shelter, and protection. This is not a particular issue in the cities, where people at this point do not have all that much anyway. It has not gone well in outlying areas, though, and I understand many civilians have been killed trying to defend their homes and supplies.

"I know many of you are wondering about the nuke at Bragg. I don't have any specific information, but the Joint Chiefs tell me that from the satellite pictures, they believe the bomb was a smaller one, and that it landed near FORSCOM headquarters. Of course, that's just a guess, as there is still a lot of smoke and debris interfering with the images. Eventually, we will get clearer pictures, and when that happens, I will let you know. The fallout cloud is expected to move towards the coast since the prevailing winds are out of the west. That means many of the towns between Bragg and the coast will experience pretty high radiation levels. In a few weeks when the radiation has dissipated, I expect we will be tasked with humanitarian missions to that area to try to help survivors.

"The EMP we experienced was not part of the nuclear blast at Bragg. Again, our satellites reported a blast at very high altitude over Kansas. Right now, we do not know who set that off, but the Joint Chiefs believe that it was a coincidence that the nuke at Bragg went off right before the EMP. One theory is another country set off the EMP and Homeland did not know it was going to happen. We don't know who, and right now it doesn't much matter. The Joint Chiefs have people investigating who set it off and will let us know when they figure it out.

"Surprisingly, there is not a lot of fighting going on in the rest of the country. Chinese UN troops have about taken over California, along with their Homeland counterparts. There have been skirmishes along the borders with Arizona, Nevada and Oregon, but we have Patriot troops along those borders to keep the Chinese and Homeland there in check. Homeland has tried landing troops on the Gulf Coast near Galveston, but the Navy and the Texas militia wiped them out. We are now in complete control of all US Navy vessels. The navy has a blockade in place for most of the ports on the East Coast, and on the coast off of Los Angeles and San Francisco. There is some fighting going on around San Diego and the southern border of California and Mexico, but the Navy and the Marines from Camp Pendleton are handling that.

"The next few days will be incredibly busy as we get set up and begin planning for the long term. I am expecting a contingent from the Air Force to arrive soon, and they will help bolster our defenses here by getting radar working again and bringing in troops and supplies. We have several companies deployed around the area for security, and nobody comes on or off base without permission.

"I want you to pay particular attention to your troops. Since almost all of the troops here are from Bragg, the nuke has got to be hitting some of them hard as they realize there will be friends and even family members who did not make it. After all, none of us have ever experienced a nuke on American soil before. Watch for any signs of stress and try to catch it early. Keep them busy, but don't overwork anyone."

General McPherson spent another hour with the officers, answering questions and making notes on issues they were having or supplies they needed. Finally, at 2130, the General kicked them all out, telling them to get a well-deserved good night's sleep.

CHAPTER SIX

Tuesday morning dawned bright and warm. The people going to Riverdale were really excited to be headed off the farm for a little while. I have to admit that I was getting excited, too. It had been a week since our trip to Whispering Willows to see what needed to be done, and I was looking forward to seeing if the eight soldiers who had stayed behind at the school were able to accomplish anything during that time. I was also looking forward to visiting with our new friends from the church. Of course, we were all excited at the thought of getting the new community put back together. Janet and Maria had packed a lunch for everyone, and we filled several coolers with cold water. We were taking six of our teens with us, and they were beyond excited that they were allowed to come with us on this trip. They were busy helping load tools and building materials into the MRAP parked in front of the house. Although we were going to work on the houses, everyone was armed, even the boys. Jimbo, Top and Scooter were doing last minute checks of weapons and ammunition, and the three of them planned to come with us to help with the work.

Finally, all the tools, supplies and food were loaded, and it was time to go. It would be a tight squeeze, but we all decided to try to ride in the back of the deuce-and-a-half truck. Kiara, Lionel, Marty, Jose, and Tim sat on the bench on one side, while Marcie, Red, Tom and I sat on the other side. The boys sat on the floor in the middle and could not have been happier. The young teens had bonded well with Red, who at 23 was not all that much older than them. Jimbo and Scooter hopped into the cab of the truck while Top drove the MRAP full of tools and supplies. We were not going far, and we would meet a second MRAP at the gate to the outer berm. That

MRAP would hold the troops who would be our security while we were working.

It took about a half an hour to get to Whispering Willow subdivision, and the whole way the boys and Red were busy teasing and razzing each other.

"Hey, Red," called Jer. "What's red and really bad for your teeth?"

"I dunno," answered Red. "What is it?"

"A brick", answered Jer, laughing hysterically.

"Okay, that's a good one," answered Red, rolling his eyes. "What do baseball teams and muffins have in common?" Red started laughing as the boys all looked at each other not knowing the answer. Suddenly, Jeff's eyes lit up. He answered,

"They both need to have a good batter!" The boys roared laughing. Then Drake, who was usually really quiet, asked,

"How do you make a kleenex dance?" At least three of the boys answered at once:

"Put a little boogey in it!"

The adults were busy laughing just listening to them. It was so refreshing to hear kids just being kids in spite of everything going on. Amid all of the laughter, we quickly reached the subdivision. Mark and two soldiers were waiting for us at the gate. After we all drove through, they re-locked the gate and followed us back to the school. Once we arrived, we all climbed out of the vehicles and looked around. I was really impressed with the work that the resident security group had gotten done. The grass around the front of the school had been cut and raked and several large compost piles had been started. All of the trash we had seen around the school was gone, and the broken windows we saw the first time we were there had been boarded up. Mark called us all into the cafeteria and gathered us around the map. I was happy to see the five families from the church were in the cafeteria waiting for us. I was even happier to see that the inside of the school appeared to be much cleaner.

Mark introduced the five families to everyone, and explained they decided they would rather stay in the school for now with the security group than in the church. The men spent the last five days moving their supplies to a couple of classrooms while the women got busy cleaning the rooms they would use.

"Okay, folks, let's get down to business," Mark said. "Gather around and let me show you where we will be working on the map." He pointed to a large map on the bulletin board behind him. "We are going to start on the block just to the north of the school. There are nine houses on that block. One home burned and there is probably not anything there worth salvaging. This one is probably too damaged to be used for human habitation. Tom, look at that one and see if we can make it into a barn or a storage building, or if we should just take it apart for raw material.

"The guys already emptied out each house of most of the furniture, dishes, clothes and stuff. The good things were sorted and put into classrooms, and the trash was piled into an empty lot on the far side of the community. We tried to completely empty each house, so we know what needs to be done."

Remembering the contents of several of the homes from our last visit, I gave an involuntary shudder. Mark apparently saw the look on my face, and explained, "We've also removed any human remains from these homes, and we now have a cemetery over by the church. We also left windows open where necessary to air those houses out. Let's divide into two groups, one on each side of the street. Security troops, post a lookout at each end of the block and the rest of you spread out to form a perimeter. All of you need to keep your eyes open. Just because we have not seen anyone here this past week does not mean there are no other people here."

I was very impressed to see that the map now listed names next to many of the homes, as well as the number and ages of children. I pointed this out to Mark and complimented the work his troops were doing. Mark laughed and said it was thanks to the three clerks with laptops that Carter arranged to go through the files. He said the three of them were not only updating the map but were also tracking everything that was brought into the school for storage and eventual distribution. They set up spreadsheets so that we would know who the original residents were, who was moved into that house, and what supplies and equipment the new residents were given to set up their households. He said they were also going to track the work that each new resident did so that he could eventually set up some kind of payment scale - so many hours of work to exchange for a house, dishes, linens or other supplies. I was really impressed, especially that only three people were doing all that work. Mark just laughed and said they were his secret weapons.

When we finished looking at the maps, Mark gave last minute instructions to the security troops, as well as the troops staying behind at the school. As soon as he was done giving directions, we headed off to the houses. With all of us working together in two teams, we were able to go through all nine homes in about three hours, making lists of what each home needed to make it livable again. While we all sat in the shade of a big tree on one of the front lawns to take a break, we compared lists between the teams. The first house needed to have the front door and a couple of windows replaced, and the carpets needed to be removed with new floors put in. The second house had a hole in the roof that needed to be repaired and had some water damage to the second floor. The windows were all OK, but this house needed repairs to the doors so they could shut and lock. The third house was in relatively good shape. Other than a few bullet holes in the front of the house, everything else looked good. The fourth house was the one that was not able to be repaired. After a quick walk-through, Tom decided it was not worth trying to fix it up into a barn or storage based on the amount of damage. He explained we would take it apart carefully so that we could reuse anything and everything that was not too badly damaged. That included shingles from the parts of the roof that were not damaged, wood from the walls, plywood sheets from the floors, wiring, windows, doors; in short, anything that could be reused.

The other team reported similar results. All of the homes needed minor repairs. One home needed several windows replaced and two had damaged doors. Inside the houses, most had areas needing sheet rock repairs. All of the houses except for the two we already knew about would be able to be fixed up for new residents.

We finished our break and then decided our first order of business would be to disassemble the one house that was beyond repair. Tom suggested all of us work together to get the house torn down. He suggested we start off by a few people removing the shingles while others went inside to start pulling up the carpets and sub-flooring. Jimbo and two of the men from the church were assigned to remove the appliances and set them on the lawn. We all split up and, in a few hours, had most of the house taken apart. As we disassembled each room, we split items into separate piles. Before long, we had piles of wiring, hardware, boards, plywood, sheet rock, doors, windows, and all of the other items that goes into building a house.

Once we had a large stack of shingles removed from the house, Tom and Tim climbed up onto the roof of the house next door and began removing the shingles around the hole. As they threw the shingles down into the yard, the six boys picked them up and sorted them into two piles: reusable or trash. Once the damaged area was exposed, the two men removed the plywood sheathing and tossed it down into the yard. It had a large rotten area in the middle, so the boys carried it off to the trash pile. Luckily, the framing underneath the sheathing was still intact and did not need to be replaced. A couple of the men passed up a large sheet of plywood taken from the sub-floor of the house we were disassembling, and Tom and Tim nailed it into place. When they finished, they climbed down the ladders so Red and Marty could bring tar paper and shingles up.

Meanwhile, Kiara was checking on the external electrical hookups for each house, disconnecting the house from the grid. She checked all of the breaker boxes as well as the connections where the power lines went into each house. She explained that if they could get a good solar set-up established, she could probably hook up each house to have some electricity.

Once Tim was down off the roof, he began checking the plumbing lines in each house looking for evidence of broken pipes or leaks. Jose and Lionel, meanwhile, removed the front door from the house we were disassembling and took it down to the first house. The rest of us kept taking the house apart.

We were very careful with both the kitchen and bathroom cabinets, as we hoped to be able to reuse them, too. A couple of the men removed the bathroom fixtures, carefully setting them out on the lawn. It was almost a treasure hunt, seeing how many items we could salvage to be reused. Knowing that it may be decades before factories would reopen to make simple things like doorknobs or electric outlets was very sobering.

Finally, we disassembled as much as we could and there was very little left of the house. Red and Marty were still on the roof next door and had just finished putting down the tar paper. Most of us decided to sit down to take a break and watch the guys on the roof. Once tar paper was laid over the bare plywood, it was time to start shingling. The boys all wanted to climb up on the roof, but Marty and Red said that would be too dangerous. Instead, the two men suggested a competition to see which team could place the most shingles on the roof. Each man paired up with three of the boys. One boy would stand on the ground and pass shingles to the next boy, who would stand part way up the ladder. He would then pass to the third boy standing towards the top of the ladder. The boy on the top of the ladder would then pass the shingles to Marty or Red. Jer, Mike, and Nate teamed up with Marty, and Jeff, Drake, and Sam teamed up with Red. Tom stopped working long enough to be the timekeeper.

"On your mark, get set, go!" yelled Tom. The boys were having a great time, with a lot of laughter and trash-talking as they raced to pass the shingles. It took about twenty minutes to finish the roof, and Red finished about a minute before Marty, using just two shingles more than Marty. As the boys jumped and yelled, Red stood up on the ridge of the roof with his arms raised.

"We are the champions!" Red yelled. Marty's team all booed and hissed.

"We are the champions of the world!" Red yelled. Jeff, Drake, and Sam were all cheering. Suddenly, several loud cracks filled the air, and Red slowly tumbled down the side of the roof towards Jeff on the ladder. Marty was just beginning to go down his ladder and tried to catch Red, but just couldn't reach. Jeff grabbed hold of Red's shirt but was not able to hold Red's weight. As the shirt began to tear, Red dropped from the ladder to the ground while the rest of the boys looked on in horror. Tom raced over to Red, and it was immediately obvious that Red was dead with several gunshots though his chest.

All of a sudden, our security team opened fire, and we were in the middle of a raging gun battle. At the same time, we heard Kiara scream. Tom ran to her and helped Kiara into the house she was working on. I pulled out my radio and called for the security team back at the school.

"We need help. Red's been shot, and we do not know where the shooters are. I think they're off to the east, but I don't know where."

A minute later, the security Humvee came tearing around the corner. Mark and Top climbed out of the front seat and ran to Red. They stopped short when they got close to the body and looked at me. I just shook my head. Mark turned to the other soldiers with him and gave them instructions to find the gunman. Top knelt down next to Red and shook his head. "This is going to tear Lynn apart, I'm afraid. She is just barely over him getting shot the first time, and now this." He looked up at me with sad eyes and said, "I want to be the one to tell her. I don't want anyone else to have to do that."

"I'm so sorry Top, and you're right – you can comfort Lynn better than any of us. We'll take care of getting a grave dug, I guess up on the hill with Grandma and Grandpa, while you take care of Lynn." I just did not know what to say. We went from having a wonderful time to being grief-stricken in a matter of minutes, and I know we were all in shock.

Meanwhile, Marty gathered the boys and brought them into the house to take cover. The older boys were angry and wanted to go find the shooter and kill him. The younger boys were terrified and both Mike and Drake looked almost tearful. Sam just looked at Marty and asked, "Dad, how are we going to tell Miss Lynn her brother was shot again? And that he is dead this time?" Marty put his arms around his son, and all the boys huddled closer to Marty.

Mark ran to the MRAP parked on the street and drove right up to the door of the house Kiara was in. Tom helped Kiara into the MRAP and Mark drove to where Lionel was waiting frantically to check on Kiara.

Meanwhile, we were still hearing sporadic gunshots as our guys went after the shooters. The battle lasted about twenty minutes, although it seemed like hours. When we finally decided it was safe, we all ran to the house where Lionel was caring for the injured. Kiara was shot, but fortunately, it was a through-and-through injury to her upper leg. Lionel was busy cleaning the exit wound, which was significantly larger than the entrance wound. He said that he would need James to help him surgically clean the wound once we got back, as there were probably fibers in the wound from Kiara's jeans. John, one of the men from the church, was also shot, but he was in much worse condition, having been shot through the shoulder. His arm appeared dislocated at the shoulder and was starting to swell badly. Lionel had already cleaned and dressed the wound as best as he could and said he would need to come back to the infirmary at the farm to have surgery, too, or else he was sure to lose the arm. Tom also had been creased by a bullet on his upper left arm and had a bandanna wrapped around it. I pulled him off to the side and told him to let me dress his wound. He tried to shrug it off as nothing, until I reminded him that without hospitals and pharmacies, any injury could turn into a lethal infection. After that, he got quiet and allowed me to clean the wound on his arm. Fortunately, it was not deep, and I figured it would heal in a week or two if he kept it clean and let me change the dressing every day.

We spent the rest of the afternoon in the house waiting for the troops to come back from chasing the shooters. Around four o'clock, we heard the vehicles approaching. Mark went out to the hummer and learned they shot four of the shooters and captured one, but at least one got away.

I was devastated to learn that in the course of capturing the one shooter, PVT Cooper was shot and killed. I wanted to go out to the Humvee and kill the prisoner tied to the front hood of the vehicle, but Mark stopped me.

"We need information. We are taking him back to the school to interrogate him. When we are done, we will have a military trial and decide his fate."

"Where is Private Cooper?"

"A couple of the guys went to get a truck to go get him. We are going to bury him here at the school. He died for this community, and it is fitting that he should be allowed to rest here." Mark rubbed his face, his eyes welling up just a bit. "He was so excited to be a part of the reconstruction. It's really all he could talk about: getting this community back to normal and seeing families move back in. Geeze, he was just a kid himself, but he talked about one of these days fixing a house up here for himself and maybe having a family of his own. He was such a good kid." Mark got silent and turned away for a few minutes.

Suddenly, he turned back to us. "Gather everyone up and let's get back to the school. There's a lot we need to do before we head back to the farm. I'll send one of the vehicles back for Kiara and John. Lionel, will you stay with them?"

Lionel looked at Mark as though he were crazy. "Of course I'll stay with these two. Where did you think I would go?"

Mark gave a tired smile. "Thanks, man. I just want to be sure these two are taken care of." He then looked at Marcie and me. "Can you two take care of cleaning up Red a little and maybe wrapping him up in a tarp or something? I don't want Lynn to see him like this." Marcie and I by now were both in tears, but we agreed to take care of Red.

An hour later, all of us were back at the school. Several of the soldiers had already dug a hole in the school yard. They chose a pretty area, with several trees and a concrete bench nearby. We all gathered around as several of the soldiers carried Private Cooper's remains out and gently placed him in the waiting grave. Mark stood at the head of the grave and bowed his head for a few minutes. When he looked back up, he looked at each of us.

"Today has been a rough day. We lost two of our own, both of them young men in their prime. And for what? For trying to make life better for the citizens of this area. They were not playing politics. They weren't trying to hurt anyone. They were only trying to help, but those cowards who shot them don't want to see anyone helping. They don't want to see anyone make this country better. They don't want to see the suffering stop. As we say goodbye to Private Nicky Cooper, remember that he died trying to help make this world a better place. He gave his life to protect yours, and in my book, that makes him a true hero. Not a movie star or a football player kind of "hero", but a young man willing to do what it takes to make this world a better place. We will all grieve his loss, but we also need to celebrate his life, and continue to do whatever we can to defeat those killers and take our country back. It's what Coop wanted." Mark suddenly stopped talking and grabbed the shovel. He scooped up some dirt and tossed it into the grave. He then handed the shovel to the person next to him. All of us took a turn silently putting a shovel full of dirt into the grave and then passing the shovel. After everyone had a turn, we all turned and went back into the school. Two soldiers stayed behind and finished filling in the grave.

CHAPTER SEVEN

It was a very sad and quiet group that pulled into the outer berm of the farm that evening. Top went on ahead to find Lynn and break the news to her about her brother. Scooter drove the truck carrying Kiara, John, and Lionel over to the clinic. Marty, Tim, Jose, and Marcie decided to walk back to the house with the boys. They wanted to walk slowly so that Top would have time to talk to Lynn before anyone else saw that we were back.

"Tom, I want you to come with me to the clinic please. We need to do a better job cleaning your arm, and we need to check on Kiara and John." Tom nodded and put his good arm around my shoulder as we walked. I knew we needed to stay busy or else the reality of the day would sink in. There would be enough time to break down later this evening after we broke the news to the rest of the farm family.

The clinic was crazy busy when we got there. James was busy working with John's shoulder injury. He called Clark in to help. Even though Clark was a veterinarian, James needed assistance with the repair, and Lionel was tied up working with Kiara. I was glad to see Amy, Samantha, and Maureen were also helping. I pulled Tom over to the only empty corner of the clinic and had him sit down while I scrubbed up and got the supplies we needed to clean and properly dress his wound. It only took about fifteen minutes, and we were done. Before I let Tom leave to go check on the others, I gave him a shot of antibiotics and told him he could not do any work with that arm for at least a couple of days. He smiled, thanked me and gave me a kiss on the forehead before leaving the clinic.

After Tom left, I scrubbed up again and went to see who I could help. Most everyone was busy helping James, so I went over to Lionel and Amy, who were working on Kiara's exit wound. They had flushed the wound well, and Lionel was now stitching it up.

"Can I help?" I asked.

"We have this under control right now. Would you go check on John's wife? I think her name is Lois. She rode back in the truck with us and is probably waiting outside." I nodded and left the clinic. At first, I didn't see anyone, but then I noticed a young woman sitting on the ground against the side of the building. She had obviously been crying. I sat down next to her and told her that they were still working on her husband, but that they were almost done, and he seemed to be doing OK.

"Is he going to lose his arm?" she asked.

"It doesn't look like it, based on what the doctors were doing. As I was coming out here they told me to tell you just that he was doing well, and you could probably come see him in about an hour."

"Oh, thank goodness. I've been so worried. I left the kids back at the school with my sister, and I was scared I'd have to go back and tell them their daddy lost his arm… or worse. I can't thank all of you enough for taking care of John."

I wasn't sure exactly what to say. "I can't tell you it is our pleasure, because nobody can take pleasure in what happened today. I will tell you I am very grateful we have the resources we needed, including doctors, nurses, and medications to be able to take care of him. You mentioned kids. How many kids do you have?"

"We have three kids. Robbie is the oldest, and he is seven. Then Elaine, who is six, and Brittany is two. My sister Caroline is watching them right now until we get back. How long do you think the doctors will keep him?"

"Let's wait until they are finished, and we can ask. I'm sure they will at least keep him overnight. We can fix you up with a cot so you can stay near him if you want. It will probably take a while for him to wake up after the surgery, so I will bring you some dinner while you are waiting."

"Thank you, I totally forgot about dinner, I've been so worried. After the doctors talk to me, is there a radio I can use to call back to the school and let Caroline and the kids know what's going on?" I nodded.

"I'm sure we can get Mark to call on the military radio and give them an update."

I spent a little more time talking with Lois, in part to make sure she was okay and taken care of, but deep down, I recognized I was stalling. I knew the next place I needed to go was to see Lynn, and I was dreading having to talk to her about Red. I was more than grateful that Top was going to break the news because I just didn't know what to say. I mean, what do you say to a young woman who just lost her only living family member? Finally, though, I excused myself from Lois and headed over to Lynn's apartment. As I approached, I could hear her crying, so I knew Top told her. I stopped outside their door and said a little prayer for help to make my words comforting to Lynn. I took a deep breath and knocked on the door. Top let me in and stepped outside. I saw Lynn sitting on the couch. As soon as she saw me, she ran over and gave me a hug, crying on my shoulder. I held her for a minute or two as though she was my child. Finally, she let go, straightened up, and led me to the couch, where we both sat.

"Thank you for coming to check on us. I can't believe after all he went through that he is gone."

"Lynn, honey, I'm so sorry. It doesn't seem real, but it is."

"Were you there when...it happened?"

"Yes, we were watching the guys on the roof. They were having a contest to see who could finish their section of the roof first. Red's team won, and he was cheering his team when he was shot. It was an instant thing, and I know that he did not suffer." Lynn kept quietly crying as I talked to her. After a minute she looked up at me.

"Zoe is going to be heartbroken. She and Red were starting to get close. At least Red is with his wife and baby now. He was just starting to be able to talk about losing them without crying. At least they are all together. Has anyone talked to Zoe?"

"I don't know," I answered. "My first thought was making sure you were okay. Tom was headed back to the house to talk to everyone else."

Lynn seemed to be getting some control of her emotions. After a couple of deep breaths, she asked, "Where are we going to bury him?"

"What do you think about up on the hill near my grandparents? It is one of the prettiest areas on the whole farm."

"I think that would be perfect. Thank you for sharing your grandparents' resting place with us."

"It is our family cemetery, and Red is family. It's only right that he should be there. I am going to head over to the house. I am worried about the boys, since they were there through all of it. I also need to get some dinner for Lois, the wife of the man being worked on in the clinic. Do you want me to bring you and Top some dinner?"

"No, I think we will go over and get dinner ourselves. I can't hide away from this, and you just reminded me that I need to be around my family." I gave Lynn another hug and headed home.

Even before I got to the house, I could see groups of people scattered in the front yard and on the porch. Many were hugging, and almost everyone was tearful. Father Dan was moving between groups trying to offer support, but it was obvious that everyone was grieving. Although some in the group had already experienced loss before coming to the farm, this was our first loss here. Our little haven from all the madness in the world seemed to get just a little bit less safe, a touch less comfortable.

I saw Tom sitting on the porch with the six boys who were with us today, and I hurried over to them. This was a very traumatic event for them, and I was worried. Yes, these boys survived the attack from the motorcycle gang last winter, but that was not really the same. The gang was trying to hurt us, and none of us grieved over the deaths of gang members. Today was different. Red was a part of us and was especially important to the boys. It seemed like the boys were doing a little better than I expected. No tears at the moment, and they were telling each other stories about things they did with Red. Tom was just sitting there, listening and nodding, and occasionally laughing with the boys. As I walked up to them, everyone seemed to get quiet. That was awkward.

"Don't let me stop you guys. It sounds like you all have some really good memories to share. I just wanted to let Tom know I'm going to get Lois' dinner and then Lynn and Top will be over for dinner in a few minutes." Tom nodded okay, and I left, headed for the dining hall.

Janet saw me enter and came hurrying over to me. "Are you okay? How is Kiara and the man from Riverdale?"

"Kiara is doing fine. They were finishing up cleaning her wound as I was leaving. The other man, John, has a pretty serious injury, but James, Grant, and Samantha seem to have it under control. I actually came over to get a dinner to bring to John's wife."

"I'll put a plate together for her. You make sure you come back and eat something, too. I know how you get when you are stressed, and you forget to eat, so I will bug you until you do."

I had just a twinge of aggravation at that, but then I realized Janet cares about me and was just trying to help. "Thank you, my friend. I'll come back as soon as I take the plate to Lois and check on the folks in the clinic."

An hour later, I was back at the clinic. Kiara's treatment was finished, and Lionel had taken her back to their apartment to rest. John and Clark were done with John's surgery and Samantha was finishing up his dressing. Lois was sitting in a chair next to John, holding his hand.

"How is he doing?" I asked Samantha.

"He is doing better than I thought he would when he first came in. James and Grant were able to fix everything, so as long as John doesn't get an infection and does therapy after the incision heals, he should regain full use of his arm."

"That is great news." I turned to Lois. "I'll bet you're relieved it went so well. I brought you some dinner."

Lois smiled her thanks and took the plate I held out to her. She dragged her chair over to the desk and began to eat.

"Samantha, have you eaten yet?"

"No, but I need to stay here with him for a while until he is completely awake."

"I can do that. Go find James and get some dinner. I'll stay until one of you is ready to come back. What do I need to do?" Samantha handed me the chart and told me to just watch for bleeding and monitor vital signs and especially his breathing.

"I think I can trust you with my patient for a while. Try not to mess anything up – we have him in good shape and I expect him to be in the same shape when I get back."

"Yes ma'am." I stood up and saluted her. She left, laughing. Lois looked at me with a bit of a nervous expression on her face.

"Um, do you really know how to take care of him?" she asked, timidly.

I started to laugh. "I'm sorry, Lois. Samantha and I were just being silly. Yes, I've been a nurse for a long time and know exactly what needs to be done."

"Oh, good. I was scared for a minute there. It's hard enough to see John going through this and being in a strange place with so many people that I don't know. Thank you, though, for everything you people are doing to help us."

"It is our privilege to be able to help. We are trying to be good neighbors. If we ever want to put our society and our country together, we will all need to pitch in and help each other however we can."

"I agree with you." Lois looked resolute. "Before the collapse, people were too focused on themselves, and didn't seem to be all that interested in helping others unless it was for some politically correct popular issue. I mean, look at the issues with separating families at the border. Everyone was up in arms about that, even though it has been going on for years. It wasn't until the issue was made political that all these people started caring. And who cares about the kids when citizens wind up going to jail? I wonder what all those people are doing now. Are they helping their neighbors or did they just find something else to protest? I hope if we can ever get this country back together again, we can learn how to be nicer to each other."

"I hope so, too. We have to start somewhere, so I guess we start here. We need to get your community fixed up and settled so we can get more communities started just like it. As we start up each community, I hope that everyone working together will help people build relationships and learn to like their neighbors and care about each other. If we can do that in Riverdale, then maybe others can follow our example in other places."

"Do you think it is possible? I mean, look at what happened today when we tried to do something good. There are still evil people in the world. Will those evil people let the rest of us live in peace, or will we be fighting for the rest of our lives?" Lois looked so sad. Of course, she and John both had already been though quite a bit even before the episode today. I tried to smile and look confident as I answered.

"We will have to defeat evil. We need to be examples of how people should act, with respect and caring for each other. Instead of ignoring evil like most people did before the collapse, we will have to confront it head on and defeat it. We've made it this far, and we will continue to make it. My prayer is that our kids will eventually inherit a peaceful world."

Lois was about to answer when John suddenly groaned. In an instant, she was at his side. "John, honey, are you okay?"

John opened his eyes, still groggy from the medications he had been given. "Where am I? What happened?"

I stepped over to his cot. "Hi, John. You're at Langston Farm. You were shot today and had surgery, but you are going to be alright." John looked around, looked at Lois, smiled, and closed his eyes. I did a quick check of his vital signs, charted them, and checked his dressing. Thankfully, it looked good and I didn't see any blood leaking through.

"He will probably do that a few more times over the next hour or so as the medication wears off. Once he wakes up, he is going to hurt. By then James and Samantha will be back and James can see about giving him something for pain."

"Won't that just make him sleep more?"

"Yes, it probably will, but sleep is good for him. Sleep gives the body a chance to work on healing itself. Would you like me to bring a cot over here next to him so you can get some rest, too?"

"Yes, thank you. I didn't realize how tired I was. Now that I know he is okay, I can try to catch a nap if I won't be in the way." I moved one of the cots over close to John and handed her a blanket and pillow.

"I'll wake you up if anything changes or if he needs anything." Lois laid down and within minutes, she appeared to be asleep. I sat next to John, watching him rest. He did not appear to be in any distress, and so I just sat there quietly waiting for him to wake up. After about forty-five minutes, James and Samantha came back. I pointed to Lois asleep on the cot and handed Samantha the chart. I told her that he only woke up once and went right back to sleep and that his vitals remained stable.

"Thanks for letting us go eat," said James. "We needed a few minutes to unwind. That was some pretty massive surgery." He then explained to me that the bullet went into his chest, just missing his lung, but fracturing his collar bone. The bullet then lodged in the top of his shoulder blade, but the shoulder joint itself was damaged by pieces of bone, which probably caused the arm to be partially dislocated. There was a lot of bleeding, but thankfully, they were able to stop that quickly. The joint damage was repaired, and they were able to remove most of the bone fragments and the biggest part of the bullet. Infection was always a worry, but if he did well, he could probably go home in a couple of days.

"That's great. I'm so glad you were able to help him. I'm headed over to the house, but if you need anything, please call me." I picked up Lois' empty dinner plate and headed out the door.

I decided to make a quick stop at Kiara and Lionel's apartment. Lionel met me at the door and told me Kiara was sleeping.

"How is she doing?" I asked.

"She's in a lot of pain. James gave her some pain meds and she's out of it right now. The damage to her leg was pretty extensive, but we were able to repair most of it." Lionel looked exhausted as he talked. "I expect she's be up walking soon enough, and hopefully it won't leave too much of a scar."

"Can I do anything? Do you want me to bring you some dinner?" Lionel just shook his head.

"No, thanks, I'm going to go to bed soon. Anaya and Freddy are staying with Stacy tonight so I can just sleep."

"All right, then. Call me if you need anything." I gave Lionel a hug and turned back towards the house.

CHAPTER EIGHT

After finishing in the clinic and checking on Kiara, I went back to the house to check on everyone there. Surprisingly, the house was quiet. Tom was sitting in the living room reading, but everyone else was gone.

"Where is everyone?" I asked.

"Gone home or gone to their rooms. Everyone was pretty devastated by what happened, and I think people are just tired. Physically, mentally, emotionally worn out. Janet left a plate for you on the counter in the kitchen. She said to tell you to eat it or else she is going to come feed it to you." I grinned at the thought and retrieved the plate from the kitchen. Settling down next to Tom again, I ate the sandwich Janet left me.

"Did you see Lynn and Top at dinner? She was doing really well, all things considered, when I went to see her."

"Yes, and I was surprised at how well she is doing. She had a lot of people laughing, talking about Red when he was a kid. She is 14 years older than Red, and so she had the joy of bringing her dates home to a pesky little brother who would ask all kinds of embarrassing questions. It was good to hear her reminiscing in a positive way."

I finished my sandwich and asked Tom about funeral plans. "Well, you know we don't have any place to store a body, and so we are planning the funeral for ten o'clock tomorrow morning. Tim, Marty, and Jose are building a simple casket. We'll have a service at the church, and then go up to the hill for the burial. Your sons volunteered to dig the grave. That was nice, letting him be buried in your family plot."

"Well, Red is family, so where else would we bury him? I just hope his is the last funeral for a long, long time. Unfortunately, I don't think that will be the case – at least until we can get rid of some of the troublemakers out there."

Tom and I sat on the couch for a while, his arm around my shoulders making me feel comforted and safe. Both of us dozed on and off for a couple of hours. At three in the morning, Bill came through the living room on his way to the camera station in the basement and accidentally woke us up. He quickly reassured us that nothing was going on, he was just relieving the person on duty. Tom and I said our good nights, and we each headed off to bed.

I slept well for a while but woke up early after another nightmare. I dreamed of the church in the Whispering Willows subdivision. The cemetery had a number of new graves, fresh dirt mounded over the top of each one. Near the new graves, though, were a lot of open holes in the ground just waiting for bodies to fill them. As I looked off in the distance, there were open graves as far as I could see. Every so often, shadowy figures would drop a body into a grave and fill it in, but every time that happened, several more holes would open. When I woke up, I decided that the dream was just the result of the bodies from the subdivision, combined with Red's funeral today. I did not feel any kind of foreboding, and so I decided to put the dream out of my mind.

The morning dawned warm and sunny, with a clear sky that could only be called Carolina blue. Mark sent several of his soldiers to man the foxholes on the inner berm so that more of our people could attend the funeral. As we gathered at the church, the only people not present were Gabby, who was still on bed rest and Stacey who stayed with her. Mark even had two of his soldiers monitoring the camera station and the OP. Father Dan performed a lovely funeral service, with just the right balance of sorrow for Red's death and joyfulness for his life. After the service, we all trooped up to the cemetery on the hill. The six boys who were present at his death were pallbearers. Tim used old bicycle parts and created a wheeled cart for the casket so the boys would not have to actually carry it. Father Dan led the procession, followed by the casket, then Lynn, accompanied by Top and Zoe. They were followed by Lionel pushing Kiara in a wheelchair so she did not overuse her wounded leg, and then the rest of us. As we walked, I thought how different this funeral was compared to funerals before the collapse. The people attending today were all sincerely grieving. Nobody was there because they had to make an appearance or because they were afraid not showing up would be a social faux pas. Everyone was there because each person genuinely cared. If nothing else came of the collapse, the close relationships forged by the people living at Langston Farm was enough to give us all hope for the future.

As the service came to a close, Father Dan asked if anyone had any words they wanted to say. Zoe stepped forward and turned to face the crowd. "I just wanted to say that Red was a very kind man. He went through a lot in his life, losing his wife and baby, then getting shot. He was always smiling, though, and always had a friendly word for everyone. He was good friends with everyone, even the boys, and I am going to miss him." Tears were streaming down her face, but she maintained her dignity. Lynn stood next to her and gave the young woman a hug. She then surprised everyone by turning to address the crowd.

"From the bottom of my heart, I want to thank each and every one of you on behalf of my brother. When we arrived here, Red was badly injured both physically and mentally. He was dying of a gunshot wound, and his heart was broken after the murder of his wife and infant daughter. You took him in, nursed him back to health, and showed him that in spite of horrible circumstances, life was worth living. He did not want to live at first, but you loved him, and he loved all of you. That love saved him and motivated him to want to help people. He felt very passionate about the restoration of Whispering Willows. He told me more than once that he was so proud to be part of the group that would rebuild America rather than the group trying to destroy her. He did not live to see the project finished, but I know he will be with us in spirit. I have some news to share with all of you. Top and I will be moving to Whispering Willows in a few days." She paused and took a breath, waiting for the sudden murmuring from the crowd to die down.

"Top has been asked to oversee the formation of a militia unit there, and I am going to help finish my brother's mission. I love all of you and it will be hard to leave here, but this is something I have to do. I won't let my brother's death be in vain. I won't let evil win. I hope as we make the area safer, we will be able to come back here and visit." At that point, Lynn's voice broke, and she stopped talking. Top put his arm around her and then addressed the crowd.

"Thank you all for everything you did for Red and for us. I believe Major Schmidt wanted to make an announcement."

Mark stepped to the front of the crowd. "I've talked to the families from Whispering Willows, and they all agreed to rename the main street – that's the one the school is on – to Marvin Reddick Boulevard in Red's honor. The cross street there at the school will be renamed Nicky Cooper Avenue. One of the ladies at the school is repainting the street signs." Everyone applauded, and Lynn gave Mark a big hug.

When the crowd settled down again, Father Dan finished the burial service, saying, "We commit our brother Marvin to his final resting place, earth to earth, ashes to ashes, dust to dust. Eternal God, you allowed us to share in the life of Marvin Reddick. Before he was ours, he belonged to you. For all that Marvin has contributed to make us what we are, for the spirit of him which lives and grows in each of us, and for his life that in your love will never end, we give you thanks. As we now offer Marvin back to you, comfort us in our loneliness, strengthen us in our weakness, and give us courage to face the future unafraid. Draw those of us who remain in this life closer to one another, make us faithful servants to each another, and help us know the peace and joy which is eternal life; through Jesus Christ our Lord. Amen."

Father Dan then picked up the shovel, scooped up dirt from the pile next to the grave, and dropped it into the open grave. He handed the shovel to Lynn, and she did the same. Everyone took a turn dropping a shovelful of dirt into the grave, most people whispering a goodbye message to Red. When the last person had his turn, Father Dan then blessed the crowd and the funeral was over. As the crowd dispersed, I went over to Lynn and Top.

"I am so sorry you are going to leave us, but I completely understand. Please let me know what we can send with you to make things easier for you."

Top looked thoughtful for a few minutes, then looked at me. "You know I will be putting together a militia. Would you be willing to share a couple of the motorcycles from the gang? That would be really helpful for scouts to be able to cover more territory. We'll have to adapt them to make them a lot quieter, but we think it would help."

"Most certainly you can have some. Let me know when you are ready, and you can pick out the ones that will work best for you. Is there anything else?"

Lynn spoke up. "I think we have pretty much what we need. We will be staying at the school for now until we can get a couple more blocks of houses done. Eventually, we'll have a house there. I may think of things, but I'll see you when you come out to the subdivision, right?"

"Of course!" I gave her another hug, promised I would see her soon, and headed back to the house. Once at the house, I went to check on Gabby and Stacey. Gabby was sleeping, so Stacey and I stepped into the hall to speak. Stacey shared that she was worried about Gabby, that with all of the stress of the funeral and Kiara's injury, her blood pressure was pretty high, and she had a headache again. She said that James had been by earlier and gave her some medication to help her rest. I thanked Stacey for being such a good sister-in-law and asked her where Jon and Chris were. Stacey explained they were in the OP to relieve Mark's troops who had things to do.

"Can you take lunch up to them, Mom? I was supposed to, but we had a rough morning, and I wanted to lay down for a bit while Gabby and John Henry were both sleeping."

"Of course I can. I wanted to spend a little time with them anyway. I feel like I don't get to see much of any of you these days as busy as we are."

Fifteen minutes later, I was climbing up into the OP with lunch for Jon and Chris. They seemed glad to see me but were especially glad to see the bag of sandwiches I brought. I brought enough for all of us since I decided to stay for a while and visit with them.

"Mom, thanks for bringing us lunch. I was starving, and Chris wouldn't let me leave to get us anything to eat!"

"Jon, you are such a whiner! I told you Stacey said she would bring us something! Hey, is Stacey okay? Why didn't she bring lunch?"

"Yes, she's fine. She's going to lay down for a bit, and I wanted a chance to spend some time with the two of you."

"Oh, good," Chris said. "I'm glad you're here. We don't get to see much of you either, even though we all live in the same house. At least Jon and I get to spend time up here together."

Jon answered, "Yeah, I'm not sure what I ever did to Frank and Bill that they keep assigning me to the OP with him. I have to listen to him complain about everything for hours on end." Chris reached over and swatted his brother, making the two of them laugh. I just grinned. They may be adults, but they will always be my boys.

"Thanks for bringing our lunch, Mom." Jon said. "These peanut butter sandwiches really hit the spot, too. But you know what I really would like?"

Chris and I started laughing, because we knew exactly what the answer would be.

"Pork chop biscuits from Bojangles, with a big glass of Cheerwine, perhaps?" I asked. Jon laughed and nodded. "Sometimes I dream at night about those biscuits. Remember when we were kids and we went up to King to visit with your friend? And remember we stayed in the hotel across the street from Bojangles? I think I must have eaten about twenty of those biscuits that trip, they were so good."

Chris joined in the reminiscing. "Yeah, that was the trip we took at Christmas. Remember the Moravian sugar cookies? They were so thin you could about see through them. And we had them with that thick hot cocoa your friend's mother made."

"Oh, I remember that cocoa, it was really good. What food do you miss, Mom?"

I thought for a few minutes, and answered, "I miss eating the barbecue at that place in Lexington. Remember those great hush puppies? At least we still have sweet tea. And do you remember when we were in San Antonio, we ate at that Mexican restaurant that made the garlic shrimp fajitas? Oh, they were good, too. How about the time right after I came home from Afghanistan the first time and we went up to Arlington with your dad to see the Rangers game and ate the seven-course beef dinner at that Vietnamese restaurant?"

Jon and Chris were both smiling at the memories. "Yep, good times, Mom!"

I looked down at my peanut butter sandwich and canteen of water and knew this moment with my sons would be another good memory. After all of the grief and sadness of the past two days, I was incredibly grateful to have my two sons with me, healthy and reasonably happy. We spent a few more minutes chatting until it was time for me to go. I gave each of them hugs and told them both how much I loved them. Then, I climbed down and started my list of chores for the afternoon.

CHAPTER NINE

General McPherson was sitting at the table in his office, when Sammy came rushing in. The general looked up, alarmed at first, but relaxing when he saw the smile on Sammy's face. "Major Angelo just checked in. He went to the caves and was a bit surprised we were not there. The guards at the caves gave him directions, and he should be here soon. Apparently, he has a group of people with him."

"Did he say who the people were or how many of them?"

"No, but he indicated he had a few vehicles with him. He said his convoy ought to be here in about an hour or so."

"Excellent. I'm also expecting a group of Air Force technicians to arrive today to work on the radar capabilities. By the way, has 1LT Diamond from the farm been over to look at the wiring and the generators?"

Sammy shook his head no. "I guess you didn't hear she was shot working in the civilian community." The general turned sharply and looked at Sammy.

"How bad?"

"She'll be okay. She was shot in the leg, but it was a through and through. It did quite a bit of damage at the exit point though, so it will take her a while to recover. Luckily, the people at the farm have a decent clinic set up with two doctors and a bazillion nurses, so they were able to take care of her right away."

"Why did I not hear about this?"

"Probably because you are in the process of setting up one of the largest new bases in the southeast, working to coordinate military actions among all branches of service, and you've been living on too much coffee and not enough sleep." Sammy continued, "They also lost one of the young men from the farm and one of Major Schmidt's troops. One of the residents of the sub-division was also shot, but he was taken to the farm for surgery to repair the damage."

General McPherson shook his head. "I hope somebody captured the shooters."

"Major Schmidt's team killed all but two of them. One got away, but they captured the other one. Mark is still interrogating the prisoner. If he survives Mark's interrogation, he will bring him to us for additional questioning. He hasn't gotten a lot of information yet, but he does know the guy he captured was the leader of the sleeper group here in town. He's been wearing the guy down, though, so he may have more information by now."

The general nodded. "I want to know what he finds out as soon as it is reported. We need to get rid of any sleeper cells around here if we plan to make this area safe."

Sammy nodded. "I've got several teams out looking for them right now."

The conversation was cut short by the deep rumble of several helicopters. Sammy looked at the general and calmly remarked, "I sure hope those are our helicopters coming in."

The general stood and walked towards the door. He turned back to Sammy and explained, "They should be delivering the Air Force technicians. I think, though, that it might be a good idea to check, what do you think?"

Sammy started laughing, and said, "I think you need more coffee." The two men walked out of the building and saw four Chinook helicopters on the runway. About 80 some odd passengers had disembarked, and they were now offloading a number of crates, boxes and supplies. One of the passengers headed over to the two men. As he got closer, the general recognized Colonel Halvorson, the commander of the Air Force troops that just landed.

"Colonel," he called. "I'm glad to see you boys in blue decided to accept our party invitation!" COL Halvorson saluted the general, laughing.

"Oh, Mac, we wouldn't miss this for the world. After all, you know you army types can't manage without the Air Force to guide the way."

Seeing the surprised look on Sammy's face, Mac turned to him and said, "Sammy, let me introduce an old buddy. Kevin and I go way back. We did some training together when we were both young officers, and we've been friends ever since. Kevin Halvorson meet Sammy Iverson." The two men shook hands, and then the three of them headed into the headquarters area.

"Yep, you can tell this is an army set-up. There's no air conditioning in here," ribbed Halvorson. Mac grinned at him.

"Air conditioning? We don' need no stinkin' air conditioning," Mac said.

"And in a few days, 'stinkin' will be the operational word around here, I'm afraid," answered Sammy. The three men stopped at the coffee pot for a quick fill up, then settled around the table in the private conference area.

"So, Colonel, what did you bring with you?" Mac asked, sipping on his coffee.

"Well, I've got 52 airmen, most of whom are technicians and/or radar operators. We've also got a few air traffic controllers who will manage all flight operations at this airfield. Believe it or not, I also have a platoon of Marine Corp combat engineers who will be making improvements to the runways and will then be available for any other projects we might come up with for them. We did not bring any heavy equipment for them, but I am sure they will manage to find what they need. We also brought the equipment we will need to get the radars and tower up and running, as well as a goodly amount of groceries. When we talked on the radio, you said you had housing for my folks?"

Mac stretched out in his chair and took a long sip of coffee before answering. "We are putting troops up in the dorms from the college next door. I've also got three hangars set up with cots, enough to sleep a few hundred. Sammy, where are we putting his folks?"

"We saved three floors of one of the dorms for your airmen. They will have to share rooms, but at least they will be spared being in a tent." Sammy smiled and added, "There's not any air conditioning in the dorms, either. You are welcome to billet with your troops, or billet over here with us. We have a few extra rooms over here. What kind of command staff do you have?"

"We don't have much. I think there are a total of nine officers out of the bunch with me today. My orders were to follow your orders. Seems like in the current Patriot military, there's not a whole lot of distinction between the branches anymore." Kevin got an evil grin on his face. "Too bad we don't have any sailors here. The navy always makes sure they have ice cream machines."

The three men started laughing and relaxed for a few minutes before Sammy excused himself to go show the Air Force to their quarters. After Sammy left, Kevin and Mac got serious and Mac started explaining the setup of the base and his plans for how they would all work together.

CHAPTER TEN

Major Lucas Angelo was exhausted as he led his convoy through the gates of the Riverdale Airport. A military policeman accompanied them to the Headquarters building, and the convoy was told to wait while the MP went in to let BG Iverson know they had arrived. Sammy was accompanied by General McPherson, and both generals were very happy to see Angelo and his men. They wanted him to come in and tell them what he saw, but Angelo asked if the people with him could be given a place to rest and a meal, first. Sammy signaled one of his aides and instructed him to take the entire convoy for now to the reception hangar and let everyone grab a nap and something to eat.

Angelo thanked Mac and Sammy and went into the Headquarters building with them. While Sammy got the coffee pot and several cups, Mac led Angelo into the conference room. "Start at the beginning and tell us what happened. Why didn't you just follow us out?" the general asked.

Angelo looked a little bit embarrassed and said, "I had too many supplies stashed in my basement to just leave them behind, so we decided to make a quick stop at the house and load up." He was quiet for a moment as he collected his thoughts.

"We were at my house in Fayetteville near the airport when it happened. Most of us were in the basement when the bomb detonated. We had two men on ground level to keep watch while the rest of us carried supplies up from the basement. When the bomb went off, the sound was so incredibly loud, it left all of us with ringing in our ears." He stopped and looked at General McPherson with a look of shock. "I never expected Homeland to actually use a nuke on fellow Americans. I expected it to be Iran or some other enemy state, not an American agency. Luckily, I was prepared. I used my Geiger counter and was surprised and very relieved to see the radiation levels were at or near normal. The guys and I talked for a few minutes and decided it would be best to continue loading supplies and head to the caves rather than shelter in place. We had four deuce-and-a-halfs, and we needed all four because of all the supplies I had stashed. While the men continued to load, I went through the house and gathered personal belongings I wanted to keep – things like childhood pictures, music, and of course, my personal firearm collection. It took a couple of hours, but eventually the house was emptied of everything we thought we could use. I know I'll probably never see that house again.

"As we finished loading, several vehicles approached. One was a Humvee, and the others were civilian vehicles. They were overloaded with supplies and packed with people. The driver of the Humvee jumped out I recognized him as a staff sergeant from the 82nd who was my neighbor from up the road. I told him I thought Homeland just nuked us, and it was time to get out of Dodge. He asked if he could follow us since there is strength in numbers and they had some wives and kids with them.

"I agreed to allow the others to follow us, but suggested they have the civilian vehicles right behind us, and then bring up the rear with the hummer. After all, we had no idea what we would run into on the road. I explained to them that I expected all of them to follow our directions, but if they wanted to split off from us, that's fine. They agreed, and so we headed out. I had the Geiger counter on the seat beside me, and so far, the readings were staying in the normal range. We had just turned onto 401 west when I noticed two of the civilian vehicles slowing down and pulling off the road. I pulled off to the side of the road and called over the radio for the men to form a security perimeter so I could find out what was going on. I walked back to the first of the stopped vehicles and asked the driver why they pulled off. He told me the car just stopped. No warning, a full tank of gas, and a fairly new battery. Radio stopped, power steering quit, no brakes. The second driver said the same thing. That's when I realized we had also been hit with an EMP. The timing was off, though, so I figured it was two separate events. I explained this to the two drivers and told them we would need to move their things into other vehicles. We didn't have a lot of room, so I explained if they wanted to be able to keep everything, we might have to find a couple of trailers. The second driver told us he worked about two blocks from where we were stopped, and he knew they had several trailers behind their building. I assigned the staff sergeant and one of my guys to take the second driver in the Humvee to his workplace and bring the trailers back. While they were gone, we all pulled into a parking lot. We pushed the two disabled vehicles up into the parking lot, too. By the time the second car was situated, the hummer was back pulling a 14-foot enclosed trailer. They detached the trailer next to the first disabled car and left to go get another. Everyone then began moving items from the disabled vehicles to the trailer. It didn't take long for the first trailer to fill up, and I have to say, I was amazed at how they had gotten so much stuff inside the two SUVs and still had room for all the people. When the second trailer arrived, I directed the family with the truck to load their supplies into the trailer to make room for all the people that were in the two disabled vehicles. Soon the second trailer was also loaded and hitched to a deuce. It was a tight fit, but everyone was able to find a place to ride. I wound up with one of the drivers of the disabled cars riding with me. Finally, we got back on the road, headed west. It was approaching two in the morning when we reached the cut-off that would take us up to Plank Road. So far, we had not seen any signs of violence or looting, but it was still early, and I knew the people around us were probably still in shock from the nuke. I told everyone to keep their eyes peeled, as they would be going through a housing development to get to Plank Road, and once on Plank, we would be speeding up. Of course, speeding up meant we would be able to get to about 35 miles per hour because of all of the cars stopped haphazardly in the road. I hoped to make it to an area just past Mott Lake where we could stop and rest. I planned to drive at night and rest during the day to avoid winding up in the middle of anything.

"Mott Lake was empty when we got to the campgrounds. It was still too cool at night for the campground to be busy. I deployed several troops to secure the area, and then all vehicles pulled in. The men quickly erected a shelter of sorts made from tarps hooked onto the sides of the trucks. I told everyone to eat something and try to sleep for a while. My plan was for us to leave at sunset and try to make it to the Uwharrie National Forest by morning. I planned for us to stop at the training site there and stay with the guys who run the site.

"We were on the road and ready to go by sunset and arrived at the training site just before dawn. Luckily, they had protected radios and I was able to contact them before we got to the site. Bear had the gates open and ready for us when we got there. The guys were great and put us all up for the day. While the rest of the folks were sleeping, I met with Sasquatch and Vulture. Sasquatch wanted to know if we had done any kind of damage assessment before we left Bragg. I told him I didn't have the equipment, and even if I did, I couldn't put all the civilians at risk trying that. Vulture told me they did have the equipment and suggested the three of us go. His exact words were 'We can put a nice report together for General Mac, and then you can come back and finish escorting these people to the caves.' To make a long story short, we left Devin in charge of my people and Sasquatch, Vulture and I hopped into their MRAP and headed back to Bragg. Please don't ask me where they got the MOPP gear – I didn't ask, and they didn't offer.

"There was not really anything to see until we got close to Cape Fear Medical Center on the southwestern side of Fayetteville. The area around the hospital was crowded with people, many of whom were injured. With no power, the hospital was dark, but they were using the parking lot for triage. As we got closer, people started banging on the MRAP, demanding a ride. We quickly drove away from the hospital and took back roads until we reached the All-American Freeway. Vulture drove until the probe for the Geiger counter hanging outside the window began to click. At that point, we stopped, donned our protective equipment, pulled the probe back into the vehicle, and sealed the MRAP to keep any smoke or fallout out of the vehicle.

"The drive onto Fort Bragg was . . . devastating." Angelo stopped and closed his eyes for a moment. "We could not recognize anything, there was so much damage. When we reached what we thought was the intersection of Gruber Road and the All-American, there was nothing but debris everywhere. There were a few brick buildings standing, but they were heavily damaged. Anything wood was flattened. We turned on Gruber towards the Special Warfare Center but couldn't see anything. Between the destruction, the smoke, and the debris covering the road, we couldn't recognize anything. We went back to the All-American and tried going towards Womack Army Medical Center. Again, nothing but debris. We couldn't even see the outline of the hospital. I think it is just...gone. Reilly Road was impassable; even in a combat vehicle we couldn't get through. In addition, there were fires burning everywhere, so we headed back towards Fayetteville. One of the things we saw that really stuck with me was a flag pole in front of one of the damaged buildings we passed. The building was burning, the flagpole was tipped at a funny angle, but the flag. . ."

Angelo's voice wavered, and he took a deep breath. "The flag was tattered, but it was still flying." He paused again and swallowed hard.

"Now I know how Francis Scott Key felt. We left Bragg and went back to Fayetteville. Downtown looked relatively unscathed, although there were many fires burning in various places in the city. We tried to head down Bragg Boulevard towards Spring Lake, but the Geiger counter was going crazy and there was an incredible amount of destruction. Pope Field, Fort Bragg, Spring Lake - I think all of them are just memories now. On the way back here, we stopped at Mott Lake and washed the MRAP down with soap and water from the lake in order to try to decontaminate it. Then we washed the MOPP gear the same way and packed it into a metal box in the back of the MRAP.

"We got back to the training site late that night. The rest of the instructors at the site had arrived and several of them brought their families. They decided to come back to the caves with us. Even though they are all retired special forces troops, they want back in the action. They say that if we can find a safe place for their families, they will all volunteer to go kick some homeland as... er...butt. We loaded up everything possible from the training site and headed to the caves. We fount LT Evans at the caves and he directed us here. So, now we are here, and we've got a large group of really angry men ready to go heap some hurting on those Homeland traitors." Angelo sat back, even more exhausted from retelling the story. He knew the general would have questions.

"Tell us about casualties," the general probed.

"We saw a lot of bodies on Bragg. From the time we first noticed radiation on the All-American until we headed back to Fayetteville, we did not see a single living person. In Fayetteville, especially around the hospital, we saw many injured. Most appeared to be burned, but there were a significant number of victims with traumatic injuries as well. Honestly, we knew we could not help them, and so after seeing them the first time, we tried not to look, especially the kids."

"Was there much of a civilian emergency response?" asked Sammy.

"We saw a number of police cars and ambulances near the hospital, but none seemed to be working. The hospital staff looked like they were doing a heroic job dealing with the victims, but there were so many. I suspect that as they run out of supplies to treat people, things will get ugly."

Mac turned to Sammy. "The people of Fayetteville have always been good to the troops at Bragg. I think we will need to return the favor. Let's see about putting together a group to go and set up relief stations. We should be able to provide medical support and probably some assistance to shelters - maybe some kind of soup kitchen support. It needs to be short term, until the people of Fayetteville can start helping themselves. We probably ought to send some civil affairs staff out there to help support local government get re-established. Will you take care of that, Sammy?"

"Of course." Sammy pulled out a small notebook and jotted some notes. General McPherson then turned back to Major Angelo.

"How many people did you bring with you?"

Angelo had to stop and think. "Let's see, there were 21 of my guys plus me. Then, we had four neighbor families. That was eleven adults and about ten or eleven kids. All fourteen instructors from the Ranger training site came with us, and they brought their families, too. That would be another eight or nine adults and fourteen or fifteen kids. I'm so tired, though, I can't even add up the numbers in my head, so I'll say somewhere around eighty people, I guess. We also brought a lot of supplies, both the stuff from my basement and all the stuff from the training site. It's a good thing their trucks still worked after the EMP because we had a LOT of stuff."

General McPherson nodded, and then looked at Angelo, who was fighting sleep. "Angelo, you look exhausted. Why don't you head over to the reception area and get some rest? In the morning, we'll see about getting everyone settled."

"Thanks, General. I am beyond exhausted at this point." As he stood up to leave, General McPherson called him back.

"I just wanted to tell you good job bringing all those civilians back." Angelo gave him a very tired smile, saluted, and headed off to get some desperately-needed rest.

CHAPTER ELEVEN

The week following the funeral was quiet at the farm. We had all been shaken to the core by Red's death. Small groups made a couple of short trips in to Whispering Willows, but always under heavy guard. They were making progress getting houses ready, and three families had already settled into new homes. John's shoulder was starting to heal, and he and Lois went back to Whispering Willows. As soon as there were two houses ready next door to each other, Lois, John and their kids would move into one, and Lois' sister Caroline and her family would move into the other. I went out twice to help get their gardens ready. We spent time looking in already-established gardens and found a lot of volunteer plants things planted the year before that came back without help this year. In fact, all three of the newly occupied homes had volunteer gardens. It did not take too many hours to clean out each garden and transplant more volunteer plants from other gardens. If they could keep the gardens healthy, each family would be rewarded with a good crop of vegetables.

One of the other things we did while I was there was look at all of the trees for several blocks in each direction from the school. We noted which ones were fruit trees and which were nut trees and marked each one on the map. As the community expanded, additional blocks would be checked, and those trees added to the map.

Later this summer, we would know exactly where to look to harvest fruit and nuts to put up for the winter.

Back at the farm, I got busy on our garden. We expanded it to be several acres in size and planted more vegetables than I could even imagine. I hoped we would have a good crop, as the veggies we put up last fall were close to being used up. I enjoyed working in the garden. For me, it was therapy. The garden has always been a place of refuge for me; a place I can come to be alone with my thoughts and work problems out in my mind. I had so many things on my mind right now that I really needed to be out digging in the dirt. First, I was worried about Gabby. Her blood pressure continued to be very variable- sometimes soaring high and other times being almost normal. James and Lionel were watching her very closely. Neither one wanted to have to do a Cesarean Section in our primitive medical conditions, so they were trying to ease her to her due date and hope for a natural delivery. I was also worried about the people going to the sub-division. Lynn and Top were planning to move tomorrow. I knew we would all miss both of them very much, and I was worried for Lynn's safety at the school. I was really surprised at the transformation in Lynn since her brother died. She had been a very quiet, passive type of person, always willing to help but rarely initiating projects. All of a sudden, she is bound and determined to help with the sub-division restoration and has been working on plans with Top of things to be done to improve and maintain living conditions there. I hoped they would be able to grow enough food to support all of them, because we could not continue to send food to them if we wanted to keep all of us fed.

Thinking about food made me think of our own fields. Andrew and his farmers-in-training had planted many acres in corn, wheat, hay, and oats. I was praying that the crops did well. We needed the wheat if we wanted to continue to have bread products.

I was also worried about food. Janet, Gabby, and Maria had done an amazing job keeping all of us fed through the winter. I knew they were using strict portion control and rationing, but the way they did it, we really didn't notice. The extra food from Carter when they arrived was a Godsend, especially since we were now feeding his troops as well as all of us, but I knew it would not last forever. Last time I was in the basement storage room and root cellar, I could tell our supplies levels were dropping. We had to get those shelves filled back up or it would be a lean winter. I guess this is how the pioneers felt. All thoughts during the spring and summer were focused on getting enough food grown so we could spend all fall putting it up for winter. Then we could spend the winter planning out what to grow when spring got here again.

The kids were also on my mind. We suspended our schooling for a few days after Red's funeral, and it was hard getting all the kids to re-engage in education. We needed to keep going, though, because we would have to suspend school again when it was time to harvest and put up all of our crops.

I was in the midst of my reverie when a voice calling my name brought me back to reality. I turned and saw Anita. She looked pale, and more than a bit nervous as she approached.

"Denise, may I have a word with you please?"

"Of course," I answered. What now, I thought.

"I came to apologize for my behavior last week. I don't know what came over me to act like that." She began to cry. "I am mortified that I spoke to you and Maureen that way. Honestly, I don't even remember all the nasty things I said, but some of the other wives told me. I don't know what happened. It's like the world around me just…broke or something. It seemed like my whole world was falling in and everything we had ever dreamed about having was fading away. I really am not like the person I was being. I think that I was just so depressed at everything we lost that I became someone I did not know – and don't want to know. Thank heavens Dr. James started me on medication. For the first time in a long time, I am feeling more normal, more human, more like me. I am also spending time talking with Father Dan, and he is helping me understand how to cope with our new reality. Will you please forgive me for being such a monster?"

I smiled tiredly at Anita. "Of course. I understand that people react differently to pressure, and God knows we have been under constant pressure since all of this started. You are not a monster, just a very overwhelmed young woman."

"Thank you." She hesitated. "I was wondering. . . could I help in the garden as my usual chore? I mean, I know it is your special area, but I have always enjoyed gardening and am pretty good at it. I think if I could have a routine job instead of just signing up for stuff here and there, I would do better. Could I? I don't want to intrude or anything. . ."

I started laughing. "Yes, I would be happy to have you help in the garden. I do like to come out here and think, but it would be nice to have company while I am working." Anita gave a long sigh and visibly relaxed.

"Oh, thank you. I'm going to run back to my room and grab my hat and gloves, and then if you could show me what you want me to do, I'll get busy."

"Take your time. I'll be here for a few more hours, I expect." When Anita came back, I spent time showing her our new way of gardening. Not only did we need to pull the weeds, but we needed to check each plant for bugs that could harm the tender seedlings. Bugs were dropped into a bucket with a lid, and later, we would feed those bugs to the chickens. It was tedious, but we couldn't just run down to the garden center for insecticide any more. I was pleased to see Anita industriously working her rows and not even flinching when she had to pick bugs. I was also glad to hear Father Dan was still counselling her. Perhaps she would be able to make it through this disaster after all.

Later that evening after dinner, we had an informal party for Top and Lynn, who were moving to the sub-division in the morning. We were all so happy that Lynn was coping with the loss of her brother, and we knew Top had a lot to do with her positive spirits. I was chatting with Tom and Patty when I heard someone tapping silverware against a glass. I looked up to see Top and Lynn standing in front of the room. Top cleared his throat as the room got quiet.

"Lynn and I wanted to thank all of you for this wonderful send-off, but also for the way you welcomed both of us into your home, your lives, and your hearts. I know we are only moving thirty miles away, but nowadays, that is quite a distance. We want you to know that you all will be in our thoughts daily. We also have an announcement to make. Lynn, will you do the honors?"

Lynn held her hand up in front of her. "We wanted to let you know that we got married this afternoon. Father Dan did the ceremony, and Amy, Kiara, and Lionel were our witnesses." The room burst into applause and cheers. Everyone called out to congratulate the happy couple. As the room settled down again, Lynn continued, "We did not want to have a big wedding. For one thing, it is too soon after Red's passing, but we especially did not want to cause any extra work for anyone and we knew how crazy busy everyone is these days. We knew we would be celebrating tonight, so we saved the fun for now."

People continued to congratulate Top and Lynn and then drifted back into other conversations. After a while, the conversation around Top turned to the militia he would be recruiting and training. Several people asked if recruits needed to have any special qualifications. Top thought for a second and then said, "Well, it would probably be helpful if they had weapons and knew how to use them. They'll need to be in decent physical condition to start, and above all they will need to have a strong desire to see this country returned to what the Founders intended it to be."

Jeff, Sue, and Jer were listening intently. Jeff called out, "Hey Top, we want to be your first recruits." The three stood up, and the room burst out in objections.

"You are just kids, you're not old enough to be militia," someone yelled. People yelled their agreement.

Lisa stood up and said, "Jer, you are only 17. That is too young to run off and play soldier."

Jer looked at his mother, and said, "Mom, I was only 16 when the raiders came, and I manned a foxhole and shot them. I'm not a kid any more. Neither is Jeff or Sue. We've been though things many adults could not handle and seen things many adults could not imagine. I think you would all agree that we are mature for our ages, thanks to our current situation. We have a strong desire to be a part of the solution to this mess. We three have all been though weapons training, and we know this area. A date on the calendar doesn't matter:

our ability to take orders and do what we are told is what counts. Top, where do we sign up?"

Top looked uncomfortable. He knew the kids had a point, but they were still, in his mind, kids. Suddenly, he had a thought. "You three make excellent points, and it fits in with something I've had in my mind for a while. I would like to start a militia here on the farm to train people to protect this area. You three would make the perfect start to that. The militia in town would be to fight alongside the troops wherever the troops may go. We never know if Carter or Mark will be forced to pull some of the troops from here to support troops somewhere else. Having a trained militia on the farm would mean you would not be left defenseless in the event the fighting comes closer to here. Lisa, I understand your concerns about your son and others who may be interested in participating, but truly, these kids are far more mature than many of the troops I've trained over the years. Do you have any objections to them being part of a farm defense force?"

The kids were beaming, and Lisa slowly answered, "I suppose that would be okay, but only if you train them and give them the equipment they need to keep them safe."

Top smiled, and told the three teens, "Congratulations, you will be my first three corporals in the Langston Farm Defense Force. I'll be back in a few days to swear you in and get your training started." The three teens cheered and gave each other high fives, while several of the others present shouted that they wanted to be members, too.

"Top turned to the crowd and said that anyone who was interested in being a part of the Defense Force should be at the meeting in three days when he returned. While some people looked concerned, most people were pleased with the solution Top found, and rejoined their conversations. After a while, people began drifting out to head to bed or to various duties. Finally, the only people left in the dining hall were Top, Lynn, Marcie, Frank, Tom and me. I thanked Top for being sensitive to the kids and understanding that they needed to feel like they were doing their fair share. I asked Top if he thought there was a chance the troops from here would be pulled away.

"They won't take all of them, but they may need some. There is a lot of fighting going on in northern Virginia right now. So far, the Ranger squads and the local militias seem to be holding Homeland forces back, but we're worried if Homeland breaks through that we'll need to send more troops that way. Carter sent a company of rangers up to southern Virginia this morning to try to get the locals interested in protecting themselves."

"Are the UN forces fighting with Homeland?" I asked.

"Not that we've seen. It seems they are staying in the big cities and taking care of things like soup kitchens, shelters, and law enforcement duties. We've not had a single report of UN troops involved in fighting here. Now, in California, it seems there is really no fighting, and the UN troops there who are mostly Chinese seem to be right at home."

"Well, I guess it's good that there's no fighting, but I'm not happy to have foreign troops in this country," Tom observed. Top laughed.

"I don't think anyone around here is happy about that, but as long as they are sticking to California and there is no fighting, we're not going to waste any time worrying about them. I know that Arizona, Nevada, and Oregon have troops on the border to be sure they stay in California." I just shook my head. Who would have ever dreamed we'd be worried about Chinese troops in America? I was happy, though, that the UN troops seemed to be performing support functions rather than fighting against Americans.

Frank frowned and asked, "How will your farm defense force impact our security here? I mean, we've already got security patrolling to make sure we have no trespassers. What will be different with the defense force?"

"That is a good point. The way I see it, we can do one of two things. First, we can keep security the way it is. Then, if there are trespassers or s severe threat to the farm, you can call on the defense force to provide the protection. The other thing we can do is combine the two groups. Make you the Captain of the Guard, so to speak, and train all of your security staff as well as the new recruits to be able to perform combat operations as well as security. I think that is the better idea, as it makes all of both forces able to do whatever is needed." Top paused for a moment. "I think you all need to be trained more in use of some of the larger weapons – grenades, machine guns, maybe even some air defense capabilities. The more people trained, the better. What do you think?"

Frank smiled. "I like your thinking. I was afraid you would be pulling from our security force, but in fact, you would be increasing it and making us a lot more capable than what we are right now. And, if you combine our capability to use electronic surveillance with an improved means to fight any of the bad guys that might come this way, we stand a lot better chance of surviving. Maybe we could do some joint work with the new Militia in Whispering Willows, too, teaching them some of the security techniques that have been successful for us. That way, if one or the other of us is attacked, we can help each other, and we'll already know how to work together. I like it." Frank nodded his approval to the idea. "I need to go talk to Bill, and then we'll meet with you in three days when you come back."

Top and Frank shook hands. The rest of us gathered up our things and we all said goodnight. Tomorrow morning would be here before we knew it.

CHAPTER TWELVE

It only took two days for the Air Force to get the control tower up and running. With the help of two massive generators, power was restored, and additional radar units were deployed. The Marine combat engineers went to town just hours after arriving and found the heavy equipment they needed to fix the runways. It took some work to get the equipment running, but the Marines did not let anything stand in their way. By the end of their first week in Riverdale, the existing runway had been extended to allow larger planes and fighter planes to land. They also expanded the shorter runway to allow for more helicopter parking. The non-functional planes that had been just pushed out of the hangers were dragged to a more distant area of the airport so they would not be in the way. If they couldn't eventually get them running, the plane carcasses would be taken apart for parts.

With radar working again, everyone slept a little better, knowing that they would not be surprised in the middle of the night by enemy planes roaring overhead. At least they would have some warning. With generator power, they were also able to set up sirens so that if danger was spotted, the people living on the base would have some warning.

Once all of the runways were clear and ready for business, General McPherson put the Marines to work building anti-aircraft emplacements. That took the better part of two days, but when they were done, Fort Riverdale was well protected. Finally, he had the Marines build several large shelters. He didn't think Homeland would nuke them, but he did not want to take a chance, especially with so many people in the area.

Lynn and Top quickly settled into the routines at the school in Whispering Willows. Lynn spent her days working with the other residents of the subdivision cleaning empty houses and getting them ready for new occupants. All of the families that had been living at the school were now settled into homes on the block next to the school, and there were two empty houses on that street. They were almost done with the eight houses on the next block, only three of which needed any repairs. Lynn and Top decided to remain in the school until a lot more families were settled.

After three days, Top went back to Langston Farms to begin training the Farm Militia. He was surprised that so many people showed up to join. Everyone he asked, though, told him that it was because they wanted to learn how to defend the farm. They were almost all excellent marksmen, but they needed to learn tactical movements in order to fight cohesively. Top started out quizzing them on cover and concealment. He would point to an object or a terrain feature and ask which it was. He pointed to a thicket of blackberries and asked Jeff if it was cover or concealment. Jeff quickly replied, "it is concealment because blackberries don't stop bullets."

He then pointed to a large boulder and called on Chris. Chris correctly identified it as cover, since boulders can stop bullets. He tried to trick Zoe by pointing to an old car. She had the right answer, though. "It is mostly concealment, because bullets can pass through the body. But, if you can get behind the engine block, it might be cover if the engine is thick enough to stop bullets."

Once everyone was clear on cover and concealment, Top started showing them how to walk in the woods without making noise. He showed them how to place their feet so that toes hit the ground first, and then the rest of the foot came down gently to avoid breaking leaves or twigs that could crackle or crunch. After a few hours, almost everyone was able to move through the forest without making a lot of noise.

Top left everyone with homework. He would be back in three days and would test everyone on walking in the woods carrying a rifle and pack to see who could make it through without making a lot of noise. Everyone got into the spirit of the training and vowed to practice until they got it right. Top reminded them that the ability to sneak up on the enemy hiding in the woods would be a valuable defensive tool.

Tom and I tried to get to Whispering Willows every few days to help where we could, and mostly so that the people there knew they were not alone in their struggle to get the community back together. We went the day after Top started his training and found a new guard shack at the main gate. It was not large, maybe ten feet square, but it had windows on all sides and a small wood stove. The two guards showed us how nice it was that they could still guard the gate, but they could be out of most of the cold and bad weather.

We went to the school and found Top in the cafeteria working with a group of Riverdale Militia recruits. He was accompanied by man dressed in camo and sitting in a wheelchair. The recruits were all sitting around tables with handguns disassembled in front of them. The man in the wheelchair was instructing them in the proper way to clean the weapons. We didn't want to interrupt the class, so we stepped out into the hallway and Top followed us. I commented on the man teaching the recruits, and Top answered, "That's Toad. He is one of the instructors from the Ranger training site. Lost use of his legs in Iraq, but he knows more about weapons than anyone else I know. He'll be teaching the recruits basic marksman skills and weapon handling."

I was impressed. "How did you get one of the Ranger instructors to come here? Is he from this area?"

"No," Top answered. "He was with a large group of instructors and their families that one of our units brought here after the bomb dropped. All the instructors and their families will be living here as soon as we have houses ready for them."

"Why do you call him Toad? He's a nice-looking guy, doesn't look much like a toad!" I figured it was a nick-name, but it didn't seem to match him.

"All the instructors go by nick-names. See if I can remember them all: Bear, Vulture, Rock, Sasquatch, Tiger, Doc, Flipper, Dinky (short for Dien Cai Dau, meaning crazy), Boom-Boom, Snaggle, Taz, Specter, and Beast. I think that's all of them. They use the nick-names since they work with Ranger trainees and are pretty hard on them. That way if they have to fail anyone from the program, the students don't know their real names and can't try to find them or their families. After a while, though, they were so used to the names, they continued to use them. Even the wives call them by their nick-names at this point." Top grinned, and said that having the instructors here was great, because they were helping get houses fixed up.

"How's that coming, Top? I feel bad that we haven't done that much since we started," Tom asked.

"You would not believe how fast they are fixing these houses. In addition to the fourteen instructors, we also have a big group of civilians that were evacuated from Fayetteville. They are working really hard with the folks already here to get houses ready and settled. We've also had three families who lived here before return. None of them lived near the school, but they are helping to fix up homes, too. They don't want to be so far from the school and everyone else."

I smiled. "That is wonderful. I'm so glad to see the community is growing successfully. Any problems?"

"Nah, other than needing the gardens to grow faster. We're doing okay, and our gardens are doing great, all things considered." Just then, Lynn and Lois came around the corner. I was really excited to see both of them.

"How's John's arm?" I asked Lois.

"He's doing great. Thank you so much for everything y'all did for him. He is still doing therapy of sorts, but he has almost full use of his arm. The wound is healing well, no infection, thank goodness, and we are so relieved. He's out at the observation post on the back side of the community right now. He can do that without putting too much stress on his arm."

Lynn looked happy, all things considered. She grabbed me by the arm and pulled me along with her. "Come on, Denise, I want to show you all the things we are doing here." An hour or so later, I had toured all of the supply areas in the school, met a number of the civilians now living at the school or in the community, and watched children playing on the playground. The garden was doing great, and I could see some of the early plants like lettuce were almost ready to eat. We walked down the block to see people working in yards, painting, or fixing doors and windows. It was extremely encouraging to me to see those empty houses being transformed into homes and a community coming alive again. Lynn also pointed out the new street signs with Marvin Reddick Blvd. and Nicky Cooper Avenue. I asked her if the signs bothered her.

"They did at first, but then I realized every time I looked at the sign, I could remember the positive things my brother tried to do. So, no more tears, let's just get this community up and running, right?" I was really proud of Lynn's courage in choosing such a positive attitude. We were just getting back to school when Tom came out the front door.

"Time to go, we need to get home," Tom called to me.

"Why, what's going on? Is there trouble?"

"No trouble, other than Gabby being in labor and asking for you." I gave Lynn a quick hug and hurried to the truck with Tom.

We got back to the farm just as Gabby delivered a beautiful little girl. Amelia Danielle weighed five pounds, four ounces and looked perfect in every way. Gabby looked pale and tired, but happy as she cuddled with her daughter. Jon was at her side, watching every move the baby made. Lionel, Maureen, and James were all there, and Maureen told me Gabby's labor was very quick, but Lionel gave the baby a clean bill of health. That was wonderful news. I asked Gabby how she felt, and she smiled softly.

"I feel wonderful. I am more tired than I have ever been, but I am so happy that she is healthy. I was worried with my blood pressure and all, but thanks to my wonderful doctors and nurse, we came through it all okay." She smiled at James, Lionel, and Maureen as they waved goodbye and left the room. "We named her Amelia

Danielle. Amelia for Jon's grandmother, and Danielle for my mother." Gabby looked wistful. "I'm not sure if she'll ever get to meet my mom, but at least she'll have her name." Jon took Amelia from her mother and handed her to me.

"Meet your Grandma, little girl!" Jon said. I studied my granddaughter closely. She had Jon's dark coloring, but her hair was curly like her mother. She had a cute little nose and little bow-shaped lips. Her fingers were also like her mother's – long and slender, perfect for playing the piano. After a few minutes, I kissed her on the head and handed her back to her father.

"You all need to rest now. I'll see you later," I said as I slipped out of the room.

The next few weeks passed quickly. Baby Amelia was baptized by Father Dan in a beautiful ceremony in our little church. She was dressed in the family Christening gown and looked precious with a little white ribbon in her dark curls. Gabby still looked a bit pale, but she said she was feeling better and stronger every day. After the ceremony, we all celebrated together. It was fun to see our three babies – John Henry, Chica, and Amelia – sleeping in their mothers' arms. We had to keep on making these happy moments happen to overcome the bad things happening in the world.

Top came out every few days to do more training with the farm militia. He and Frank put together a physical training program to help improve strength and endurance of all the members. Top provided all of them with M4 carbines to use instead of the assorted individual weapons. He explained that having one standard rifle meant they could share ammunition and magazines. Also, the lighter weight of the M4 was easier for some of the younger and smaller militia members. Everyone got proficient loading the magazines with the 5.56 mm rounds and passed their marksmanship tests with flying colors. They moved on to learn hand to hand fighting. In addition to traditional military combat techniques, one of the Ranger instructors was proficient with Krav Maga. Sasquatch had worked in Israel with their army for a year and learned the close combat techniques while he was there. Bill had also learned Krav Maga while he was a police officer, and the two men began teaching all of the militia members. At first, the teens were excited because they thought Krav Maga was some sort of exotic martial arts training. When Bill and Sasquatch explained it was more of a system of self-defense, they seemed almost disappointed – until they started learning some of the concepts used. I had never heard of it, but things like learning from a position of disadvantage, having a successful mindset, and learning to use the body's natural instincts made a lot of sense. It wasn't just the teens that enjoyed this training. All of the adults and even some of the soldiers had a good time learning the skills.

One challenge the Militia had was the lack of uniforms. Since they just wore various forms of mismatched camo, they did not have anything specific to distinguish them from an enemy. Stacy came to the rescue though, using some of the material we stashed away to make purple armbands to distinguish them as militia members. Top liked the idea so much, he brought it back to Whispering Willows, and their militia now had orange armbands.

Mark was great about providing us with additional weaponry. Jeff, Jer, and Sue were ecstatic when Top selected them to be trained to use the M320 grenade launchers. They were even happier when they each got to actually fire a grenade out in one of the far pastures. Fortunately, Top warned all of us beforehand, or else we would have all freaked out to hear grenades going off so close. He also provided us with a Browning M2 .50 caliber machine gun, affectionately called a "Ma Deuce." Even the adults fought for their turn to fire the M2. Top did an excellent job, not just training us to use these weapons, but giving us all the confidence to be able to fight together if we had to in order to defend the farm and each other.

After the training session, a group of us were sitting chit-chatting with Top. I asked him whatever happened to the prisoner that was taken after the battle at the sub-division. Top's face instantly took on an angry look.

"Mark got a lot of information out of him. He was a lot higher up in the Homeland echelon than just the leader of a sleeper cell. He knew all about the nuke and the EMP, and was pretty angry to find out most of Bragg was empty when they nuked us. Guess he felt like we double-crossed Homeland by evacuating before they got there."

I looked at Top in horror. "How could you let him know that? He will go back and tell Homeland and they will come here after all of us!"

Top smiled and put his hand on my arm. "Calm down. The only way he will be able to give Homeland any information is if they hold a séance to contact him."

It took me a minute to realize what he was saying. "He's dead?"

Top nodded. "Yep, shot by a firing squad after a military tribunal found him guilty."

"Oh, thank goodness. You scared me for a minute. I'm sorry, I know Mark would never do anything that would jeopardize all of us."

The community at Whispering Willows continued to grow slowly and steadily. The Marine combat engineers had been making scavenging runs all over Riverdale and found quite a few townspeople struggling to survive in basements, abandoned stores, and damaged homes. The Marines helped these people relocate to Whispering Willows where they would have a much better chance of surviving. Although the Ranger instructors were anxious to go fight Homeland troops, they knew that they were still needed to help the community grow. They made themselves as useful as possible, working hard to help new people settle in, training militia troops, and working on improvements to the community's security. Mark continued to make frequent visits to check on progress of the community and all of us looked forward to his reports of things they accomplished.

Tom and I were sitting in my office one evening when Mark came to visit. I went to the kitchen to get us all some tea. When I came back, Mark was telling Tom about a problem family in the Whispering Willows subdivision. Mark backtracked his story to catch me up.

"I was telling Tom we have quite a few new families that have moved into the sub-division. We have over thirty homes now occupied around the school. There is one family, though, that I have some concerns about. This couple showed up six nights ago. They say they are father and daughter, but they sure don't act it. They are more like boss and worker. She never asks him to do something; she always issues orders. If I didn't know better, I'd swear she is his supervisor. Sometimes it makes me wonder if there is some elder abuse going on."

"Where did they come from?" I asked.

"I'm not sure. They just showed up at the gate one day saying they were looking for a place to live. They looked so pitiful, starving and dirty, that we felt bad for them and let them in."

"Do they do their fair share of work?" Tom asked.

"That's just it. They do, but they seem to always be underfoot whenever we are trying to have a meeting or discuss anything sensitive. The daughter, Rachel, comes looking for me to ask really stupid questions or to tell me something utterly insignificant," Mark explained.

"Maybe she has the hots for you," Tom suggested.

"Oh, please, I have better taste than that. She is. . .well, she is very aggressive. Not at all like the ladies I am used to dealing with. She also always seems to be poking around in areas that she has no need to be in. For example, Taz caught her yesterday trying to get into the armory. She made the excuse that she thought that's where we stored the kids toys and she was getting ready to go play with the kids in the day care."

"How do the other ladies get along with her?" I wondered.

"They seem to try to avoid her. At first, they were really friendly and tried to help both of them, but she was just so snooty, the ladies now don't even try to interact with her."

"Has anyone spoken to her father? I mean, if you think elder abuse might be happening, maybe someone ought to look into it."

"Bear, Toad, Top and I have talked about it. Toad is going to try to talk to him. Being in the wheelchair will make him seem like he is not threatening. I swear, sometimes the old man looks terrified." Mark's face gave away his concern for the old man. I was intrigued about his mystery family and kept asking questions.

"Have you asked her anything about herself?"

"The ladies tried, but her answers seem to be very vague. Personally, she gives me the heebie-jeebies. Her eyes never stop moving, almost like she is trying to memorize everything around her," Mark said. He suddenly looked very serious. "Do you think she could be a spy for Homeland?" Tom started laughing.

"Oh, come on Mark, she is probably just a scared woman who has been though too much and is just trying to stay safe," Tom said.

I frowned, shaking my head. "I disagree, Tom. As Mark was describing her, I had the same thought. I think you need to be very careful around her. Did she have a lot of supplies with her when she came?"

Mark looked thoughtful for a minute. "I think she just had a dirty backpack, and the old man was carrying a small suitcase."

"I think you ought to question the father pretty quickly. Her behavior certainly warrants a conversation with her, too. You might want to talk to them separately just in case your suspicions are correct and she is not really his daughter. If he looks terrified at times, maybe he is not with her willingly."

"That's what I was thinking. Thanks for your suggestions. We'll talk to them both in the morning."

The three of us continued to visit for a few minutes, until Mark looked at his watch. "Oh, my, I only planned to stay for a few minutes to say hi. I need to go see my dad for a few minutes."

As Mark got up to leave, Tom and I stood up and I gave Mark a hug. "Let us know if there's anything we can do about your mystery family. We'll do whatever we can to help you. We appreciate all you've done for us."

After Mark left, Tom and I sat back down in my office. I looked at Tom and said, "I don't have a very good feeling about this."

Bear, Top, and Toad gathered in Mark's office at the school. The former principal's office was a good spot for him to get his paperwork done. Mark entered right behind the three men and shut the door to the anteroom as well as to the office. "Okay, gentlemen, I think we have a problem. I was talking with Tom and Denise last night, telling them about our concerns with this family. Denise shares my feeling that this chick might be working for Homeland. I have absolutely no proof of this, but I would rather we addressed it and were wrong, than we let it go and it comes back to bite us. First problem is I am concerned about Mr. Macintyre's safety. Rachel looks too young to be his daughter, and he looks positively terrified of her. Second problem is they both keep turning up where they really should not be. I could see if it happened once in a while, but it seems to be a constant thing. I am betting you that if you look outside the door to the anteroom, one of the two will be nearby."

Bear got up and silently opened the door to the anteroom. He walked quietly to the door to the hallway and opened it suddenly, and Rachel was standing right outside the door. She jumped as the door flew open.

"Did you need something?" Bear asked.

"Um, n-n-no, I was just um. . . passing by," Rachel answered.

"Oh, okay," Bear answered, standing in the doorway watching her. She looked at him and turned, hurrying down the hall. Bear started laughing and went back to Mark's office, closing both doors behind him.

"Well, you were right. What are we going to do?" Bear asked.

The four men looked at each other. Suddenly, Top smiled. "I have an idea," he said. The men huddled around Top while he whispered his idea. After quite a bit of discussion, the four finally put their plan together.

Several hours later, Top was outside the school and saw Rachel and her father walking out of the school towards the road. He quietly pulled out his radio and whispered, "Show time, guys." Bear came out of the school and acted surprised to see Rachel. He hurried over to her. "Rachel, wait up, do you have a minute?"

Rachel turned and saw Bear. Her initial expression was irritation, but she quickly covered that expression with one of fear. "What do you want?" she called out. By now, Bear was very close. He took off his cap, and, acting somewhat shy, said, "Well, I wanted to apologize to you for scaring you this morning. I thought I heard someone knocking on the door, and I tripped as I was opening the door, making it fly open. I just hate that I scared you doing that. I'm so sorry."

Bear could almost see the wheels turning in her head. She turned and leaned up against the stockade fence behind her. She smiled at him and said, "Thank you for apologizing. You really did scare me. I thought I did something wrong again and you were going to yell at me."

"Oh, mercy, no, I would never yell at you. Truth is, you startled me when you happened to be in the hallway. I . . . er. . .I wasn't expecting to see you. I figured it was one of the guys looking for me and knocking."

Rachel smiled, almost flirtatiously. "Well, if I knew you were in there, maybe I would have knocked." Bear moved a little closer to her, leaning up against the fence, flirting right back. "I wish you had. I would have much preferred spending time talking to you than listening to those guys drone on about stuff."

While Rachel was focused on her flirting with Bear, Top and Mark stepped from behind a truck parked on the road. They took Mr. Macintyre by the elbows, lifted him up, and carried him behind the truck. Once he was behind the truck, they whispered to him to not make a sound. They sat him in a wheelchair and quickly pushed him into the school.

Rachel, meanwhile, was busy trying to impress Bear. Suddenly, she realized her father was nowhere around. "Dad?" she called. "Dad, where are you?" She turned to Bear. "Did you see where my dad went?"

Bear answered, "No, I was paying attention to you. I'm sure he is fine and is just taking a walk or something. Where were we?"

Rachel looked agitated. "No, you don't understand. He can't be alone. I mean… um… he has dementia and is not safe by himself. I have to watch him."

Bear tried hard to look serious. "Well, let's go look for him then." He led her further down the street away from the school.

Meanwhile, Mark and Top settled Mr. Macintyre into the principal's office. Toad and Dinky were sitting at the desks in the anteroom, just in case Rachel tried to enter. Mark explained to Mr. Macintyre that they did not mean him any harm, but they were worried about him and needed to talk to him.

"I can't talk to you. I just can't." Suddenly, Mr. Macintyre began to cry.

Mark was startled by the tears. "Mr. Macintyre, why can't you talk to me? I just want to ask you a couple of questions, and then you'll be free to go."

"No, no, they are going to kill her if they think I talked to you," he said as he continued to cry.

"Kill who?" Mark asked. "Who are they going to kill?"

"It's too late. They will know I was in here and they will think I talked. Oh, Sarah, I'm so sorry."

Top knelt down next to the elderly man. "Mr. Macintyre? Who is Sarah?" he asked gently.

Mr. Macintyre looked up at him with tear-filled eyes. "My wife. Sarah is my wife. We've been married fifty-two years. We never had any kids, it was always just the two of us. She is my whole world and now she is going to die because of me."

Top looked at Mark, then turned back to Mr. Macintyre. "Isn't Rachel your daughter?"

Mr. Macintyre shook his head violently. "No. She is one of them."

"One of who? Who is Rachel?"

"She is not my daughter. She is a Homeland agent. They are holding my Sarah prisoner. The deal was if I acted like her father for a few weeks for her to complete her mission, they would let Sarah and I go. Now, I may as well be dead, because they will kill my Sarah when they find out I was with you without Rachel there to supervise us." Mr. Macintyre began crying again.

Mark squatted down next to Mr. Macintyre and put his hand on his shoulder. "Where are they holding your wife? I can send some soldiers to go rescue her if you tell us where she is."

Hope finally showed in Mr. Macintyre's eyes. "They are holding her in what used to be our house." Mark and Top continued to gently pry the information out of their guest. When they were finished, Mark took his radio and sent a message to Bear. "Bingo" is all he said.

Bear and Rachel had been walking around the block, supposedly looking for her father. Rachel became more frantic the longer they looked. Bear suspected the fear was real but continued to play his role. They were several blocks away from the school when he heard the word "Bingo" on the radio. He waited a few minutes, then said, "Rachel, why don't we go back to the school and get one of the hummers? We can make better time looking for him, and we'll be able to give him a ride home when we find him."

"I don't know about that," she waffled. "Okay, let's go." They turned around and began to walk quickly back to the school. As they approached the front entrance, Bear said, "I need to go get the keys from Top." They continued into the school. As they entered, two soldiers stepped from alongside the doors and took Rachel firmly by the arms.

"Let go of me. What do you think you are doing? Get your hands off me," she screamed. "Bear, help me."

"Oh, I've helped you enough Rachel, or whatever your name is. After all, I didn't shoot you out there."

"What are you talking about? Has everyone gone crazy? Let me go!" She began to cry. "You have to let me go because I need to find my dad. He is old and confused and might get hurt if I don't find him." She looked up at Bear, crying and trying to flirt through her tears.

"Rachel, you are a piece of work," Bear said. He addressed the soldiers holding her arms. "Cuff her and bring her to Mark's office." The two soldiers cuffed her hands behind her back and then zip tied her feet together, with Rachel yelling, screaming, and fighting with them the whole time. Finally, one of the soldiers took his sweaty, dirty bandanna from around his neck and used it to gag her. He looked at Bear and said, "Sorry, but I'm tired of hearing her yell." The two soldiers then picked her up and carried her into Mark's office, where they unceremoniously dumped her into a chair.

Mark was leaning against the front of his desk with his arms crossed. He looked first at Rachel, then at Bear. "I'm not sure which one of you is better at acting. Good job, Bear. Go see Top. He has some work for you to do."

"Roger, Mark," Bear said as he left the room.

Mark pulled a desk chair over next to Rachel and sat down. He crossed his legs and folded his arms across his chest as he watched her. She continued to try to talk through the bandanna, squirming around on the chair. Mark watched her silently for a few minutes, then reached over his desk to grab a piece of rope.

"This is to be sure you don't try to run away," he explained as he tied her to the chair. "Now, if I take that nasty bandanna off, are you going to start yelling?" She looked at him and shook her head no. He reached over and started to pull the bandanna down. As soon as he got the bandanna away from her mouth, she started yelling at him. He reached over and slapped her across the cheek, and she immediately shut up. "That is much better. Start screaming again, and you'll get the bandanna back."

She looked at him defiantly. "You do not know who you are dealing with. I am going to enjoy killing all of you."

Mark started laughing. "You think you're pretty bad, don't you? You won't be killing anything, except maybe the grass over your grave, sweetheart. Now here is how it is going to work. I will ask questions, and you will answer."

Rachel looked at him with an expression of pure loathing. "I'm not answering any of your questions. You cannot make me talk."

Mark just relaxed, grinned, and got comfortable in his chair. "Okay, I have plenty of time. First question. What is your real name?" Rachel just stared at him. Mark smiled and continued to stare back. After a few minutes, Mark told her, "You may as well just answer. I did a lot of interrogations while I was in Afghanistan and Iraq. You may think I will be nice to you just because you are female, but you'll be wrong." He continued to sit there, smiling and watching her.

After twenty minutes of silence, she spoke. "I need to use the bathroom."

Mark answered, "Okay," but did not move.

"Well, are you going to untie me so I can use the bathroom?" she demanded.

"Nope."

"What do you mean? You have to untie me or else I will have an accident right here."

"Oh well. Until you answer my questions, I am not untying you. No food, no water, no bathroom, no goo-goo eyes at Bear, nothing. Not until you talk."

An hour later, she still had not said anything. Mark got up and Top came into the room. He sat down in the chair Mark just vacated, got comfortable, and smirked at Rachel. Mark left the room while Top continued to look at Rachel. When Rachel was sure Mark was not coming right back, she tried her bathroom plea on Top, only to have Top tell her the same thing. "No talking, no bathroom, no food, no water, no sleep." Throughout the rest of the day and long into the night, Top and Mark took turns sitting with a silent Rachel. Both ate their dinner in front of her and drank several bottles of water. When she looked like she was going to sleep, they would either make their radio squeal or else blow an air horn. Finally, about a half-hour before dawn, she finally caved.

"What do you want to know?" she asked.

"Who are you, why are you here, what was your mission, who are you working for, you know, the usual questions good guys ask spies," answered Mark.

"My name is Cheryl Bates and I am General Bates' daughter."

"General Bates, THE General Bates that hates General McPherson? That General Bates?"

"Yes, that is my father. He found out that McPherson escaped from Bragg and that his nuke did not get him. That really made him angry. He sent me to get as much information as I could about McPherson's operation here. He plans to kill all of you."

"What do you mean, HIS nuke?"

"My father set up that little operation to get rid of General McPherson. He used a smaller nuke because it was just supposed to take out the Special Warfare Center and McPherson with it."

Mark shifted in his chair to get more comfortable. "So, why are you here in this subdivision?"

Cheryl took a moment to sigh and roll her eyes. "Because it is close to McPherson's new base. I tried to get onto the base, but they wouldn't let us in and sent us here instead. I figured if I hung out here, one of you would eventually slip and let me know where to find McPherson."

"How did your father know to come here to find General McPherson?"

"Satellite images – he saw the convoys leaving Bragg before the nuke dropped and followed the images here."

"Who were the men back at Mr. Macintyre's house?" Cheryl caught on to Mark's use of the past tense and sighed. "They were some of Daddy's men. I guess you found them?"

"Yes, we found them, and we rescued Sarah, too. And before you tell me it was their idea and you were just doing what you were told, they told us it was you that captured her and got her husband to agree to act as your father. Oh, and while we are talking about failed spy tactics, you should not have left all of your codes and frequencies on the table in your house next to the radio. We've been having a grand time listening to Daddy calling you and your henchmen. We let Daddy know you are safe with us, just in case he was planning on dropping another nuke. My, my, my, your daddy has quite a temper, did you know that? Of course, he did say that you being here will not stop his plans. He said if anything happened to you it would just be collateral damage from his plan of revenge against General McPherson." Cheryl began to cry, harder this time.

"Just take me outside and shoot me, then."

"As long as you are answering my questions, you are alive. Stop answering them or try to lie to me, and I may just do that."

Eight hours later, a very tired Mark walked out of the office. He got all the information he could and now needed to go report that information to General McPherson. Cheryl's tribunal would be held later that evening.

CHAPTER THIRTEEN

As summer approached, our gardens were growing well. We spent a lot of time weeding, and bug-picking, and watching our fruits and vegetables grow. The herb gardens were growing like crazy. We had already started cutting them back and drying the cuttings for use this winter. I was very pleasantly surprised to find that Anita was an excellent gardener, and she spent most of every day working in the gardens. She was also working with a few of the younger kids, teaching them how to tell the weeds from the plants. Apparently, her medications were working well, because she seemed to be quite happy out in the garden. I never did talk to Mark about her, and now I am glad that I didn't.

We had fallen into new routines centering around maintaining the farm as a safe and nurturing place for all of the people living here. We were busy maintaining the gardens, tending the fields of corn, hay, oats, and wheat, and keeping all of the animals healthy. In between such mundane tasks, we also drilled the farm militia for a couple of hours at least every other day. Top was very complimentary about the progress we made and how quickly everyone had learned the various techniques. He felt that if necessary, we would be able to integrate well with the soldiers already on the farm and would be able to defend ourselves quite well. He also reported that the Riverdale

Militia was also doing well, and he was almost comfortable that they, too, would be able to defend themselves.

Several days after Mark exposed 'Rachel' as a spy, Tom and I took a trip to Whispering Willows to meet with Mark and Top at Mark's request. Mark welcomed us into his office and after a few minutes of chatting, Mark said, "Let me cut to the chase and tell you why I wanted you to come here instead of meeting at the farm."

Tom interjected, "I was wondering about that. I figured you had an ulterior motive."

Mark grinned and continued, "As you know, we were able to rescue Sarah McIntyre and reunite her with her husband. They are staying here at the school, but this is not really a great place for an elderly couple. I was wondering if you would be willing to let them come live at the farm. Top and Lynn's apartment is still vacant, and we thought it would be a better environment for them there than here at the school." Mark paused for a moment, and I looked at Tom. Tom shrugged his shoulders, so I looked back at Mark.

"Can we meet them?" I asked.

"Of course! Come on and I'll introduce you." We found Simon and Sarah McIntyre in the day care area playing with several small children. Mark called them over to us and introduced us. Simon looked to be in his late seventies. He was not very tall and was almost bald but had intense light blue eyes. Those eyes don't miss a thing, I thought. Sarah was short and a bit on the pudgy side, a little younger-looking than her husband with neatly braided grey hair. When she smiled, her whole face lit up. She reminded me a bit of my grandmother. Mark explained to Simon and Sarah what we had in mind.

"I'm not sure I would fit in with your group," Simon said sadly.

"Why not," I asked, surprised at his response.

"Well, for one thing, I'm Jewish. I know you run a Christian farm over there and even have a church."

"You are right that we have a church, and we do try to live by Christian values. But we would never turn you away because of your religion, and we would never interfere with your practice of your religion. After all, Jesus was Jewish, too." Sarah smiled and looked relieved until Simon continued.

"I also am a registered Democrat. I didn't vote for our current president. I know that makes us the bad guys in this whole nasty event, but I've been a Democrat all my life."

I smiled and heard the echo of General McPherson's speech in the back of my head.

"I do believe our nation was founded on the principles of respectful discourse. Did you have anything to do with what those radicals in Washington did?"

Simon looked startled. "No, of course not. What they did was reprehensible."

"Well, then, it seems to me that having someone with a different political point of view will be good for us. Maybe we can teach each other a few things. I actually look forward to us having some good interesting political discussions." I paused and looked intently at Simon. "Now, are you willing to come back to the farm with us? We have a lot of kids who could really use another set of grandparents around."

Sarah was smiling widely. "Come on, Simon. Stop making excuses."

Simon smiled at Sarah. "You are good with this? Will living there make you happy?" Sarah's big smile was all the answer he needed. He stood and reached out to shake my hand. "We accept your gracious offer."

Sarah was not so formal. She jumped up and gave first me and then Tom a big hug. "Thank you from the bottom of my heart. Living here has been good, but it is hard to feel at home when you go to sleep in a classroom."

I asked Sarah, "Do you have things at your old home that you want to get to make your new home feel comfortable?"

"No, when I was rescued, we packed up everything worth keeping and brought it here."

"Well, then," I said. "That's settled. When do you want to move?"

Sarah looked timidly at Simon. "Can we go back with you today? It won't take me very long to get our things together."

"Of course!" I answered. "Let me radio the farm and tell them to get your place ready."

Tom cut in. "I'll take care of that. Why don't you go help Sarah and Simon pack their things?" I thanked Tom and the three of us headed down the hall to the room Sarah and Simon had been using.

Early summer was almost idyllic. The weather was great, the gardens were growing, and people were healthy and reasonably happy. Our frantic preparations of last fall had paid off in that we now knew we would make it until the garden came in. My two grandbabies were growing like weeds, and John Henry was even starting to crawl and babble. We were still really busy each day just keeping the farm going, but it seemed the high stress level of the last few months had dropped a bit. Tom and I were able to spend a lot more time together and our relationship was growing closer and stronger. My sons kept hinting that perhaps we needed to have another wedding soon on the farm (neither one of the boys ever really learned to be subtle) and Tom and I kept trying to ignore them.

Simon and Sarah fit in perfectly at the farm. Within days, all of the kids were calling Sarah "Bubby Sarah" and Simon became "Gramps." Sarah was the stereotypical Jewish grandmother. She spoiled the kids rotten, reading them stories, sneaking them little treats, and playing with them. She worried over them and fussed over them all. The kids loved being with Bubby and Gramps, especially the little ones.

Sarah also insisted on helping out in the kitchen. Suddenly, we were finding exotic things on the menu such as potato knishes, latke, kibbeh, and sweet rugelach. We were excited to find Simon spoke Hebrew fluently and was willing to teach, so we added Hebrew to our school curriculum. Simon also found a friend in Father Dan. The two men would sit for hours in the evenings debating the Old Testament, and just listening to them was both educational and entertaining.

We made a conscious decision to back off some on our support of the community at Whispering Willows. The community had grown enough that the residents there were doing great fixing up houses and settling new residents. Now that the community was beginning to stabilize, they were working on the little strip mall across the street from the school and hoped that by late summer they would be able to set up trade fairs so people could barter for needed items. We agreed to attend the trade fairs, especially now that the kitchen crew learned how to make some really tasty cheeses. We knew the cheese and some of our baked goods would go over well at the community since they did not yet have much in the way of farm animals.

Mark kept us up to date on what was going on at the new base in Riverdale. They were now getting planes and helicopters in on a fairly regular basis, and the base was growing quickly. I missed seeing Carter around the farm, but Mark told us he had his hands full overseeing the activities of his troops. There was not much new on the front lines. It seemed that we were at an impasse in Virginia with the Homeland troops. The Patriot troops repelled several attempted invasions, and Homeland was constantly shifting its troops around along the border. As a result, our troops were also needing to frequently adjust their positions to keep Homeland from finding a weak spot to attempt to break through. The situation in California had not changed particularly except there was an exodus of people trying to leave the state. Homeland and the Chinese UN troops did their best to keep them from leaving, but the Patriot troops on the borders were able to assist many people to escape.

While I wouldn't exactly call the end of June the lazy days of summer, the days were certainly a lot less crazy than they were when we were trying to get apartments built and adequate stores in place. Frank and Bill kept on us, though, reminding us we could not get lax with our security or our training. It was hard to get people to find the motivation to show up to drill every day because most of us were tired. We had our adrenalin running for months on end, and now that it was reasonably quiet, people wanted to rest and relax.

CHAPTER FOURTEEN

We decided to make a big deal out of the Fourth of July and planned a cookout. We had butchered a cow in late June and intentionally ground a lot of meat to make hamburgers. The kitchen crew baked buns, and we had enough potatoes to make a vat of potato salad. Although we wouldn't have a parade or fireworks, we decided we would play baseball on the front lawn and follow it with burgers. If only we had enough apples to make apple pie! It doesn't get much more American than burgers, baseball and apple pie, right? Everyone was excited because we also decided only absolutely essential work would be done that day so everyone could relax. Mark's troops took over security for the day so our people could all participate in the fun. The troops that were not on security duty, though, came over and played baseball with us. We had a wonderful time watching everyone play. The younger kids decided to be the cheerleaders and cheered every time someone actually hit the ball, no matter which team it was. By the end of nine innings, the score was tied and all the players just shook hands and decided to just call it a tie. We sat on blankets on the front lawn and ate our burgers with homemade kosher dill pickles and potato salad. Everywhere I looked, I saw people laughing and having a good time. Tom was sitting next to me and watching me watch everyone else.

"What are you looking at?" he asked.

"I am just watching everyone smiling, being happy, acting like it is not the end of the world as we knew it. . . having a good time. I'm watching our kids playing and acting like kids instead of pulling security shifts or working as hard as the adults. I'm watching our soldiers acting like young men and women instead of fighting machines. It's good to see everyone getting along and having fun."

Tom looked around at all of our extended family, enjoying the day. "Isn't that the reason why we were preppers? So that if something happened, we would still be able to have this kind of quality in our lives?"

"You're absolutely right. It was hard, but I am so glad we did everything we did. I don't know how we would have been able to survive if we were not so prepared. We need to stay prepared, though. I'm worried that it is not over yet, and it will be winter before we know it. We're not ready yet to be able to feed everyone, and I worry about the things we are running low on that we can't replace."

Tom just shook his head. "I wish you would just relax a little. The gardens are doing great, we've got a few hunts planned later this summer to get a few deer, and our animals are all healthy and doing great thanks to Clark and the girls. The field crops are growing, and we will be fine. Besides, I haven't heard that we are running low on anything."

"I worry that we are going to run low on things like soap, and what about medicine?"

"We can make soap, and Samantha and James have been working on botanical treatments to replace the chemical medications as they run out. Please stop worrying, at least for today!"

I turned to Tom and smiled. "I'm sorry, you know it is hard for me to not worry. But you're right. We need to just enjoy the day."

We sat on the lawn until the sun went down. Once it got dark, the lightening bugs came out and the kids had a blast catching them and letting them go. As we got up to go inside, I folded the blanket on which we were sitting. Tom took me by the hand and leaned over to whisper in my ear. "Instead of taking that blanket into the house, why don't we go down by the pond and sit and watch the stars come out?"

I giggled and agreed, but only if we could slip away without people seeing us. At the moment, I was glad for the EMP that kept us from having lots of lights on in the yard as we crept away. I just did not feel like putting up with the teasing that I knew would come our way if people saw us sneaking off in the dark.

The pond was not very large and grass grew all the way to the edge. The kids had been keeping the grass cut here so they could go fishing. We found a level place and spread the blanket out. Tom got up and said he would be right back. I couldn't see where he was going, so I laid back on the blanket and just admired the night sky. The stars were especially bright tonight. I guess that was another good thing about the EMP; there was no light coming from town or nearby cities, and so the stars could shine really bright. About five minutes later, Tom came back with a plastic bag. Opening the bag, he pulled out a bottle of wine and two glasses.

"Where in the world did you get that?" I asked.

"I've been saving it for a special occasion. I figured this holiday is a special occasion, especially since I got you to slow down and spend time with me." He opened the bottle and poured us each a glass. I was pleasantly surprised to find it was cool. I looked at Tom and he explained he had put it in the water at the edge of the pond to get it cool.

We sat there in the starlight drinking the wine, and I felt a sense of peace I hadn't felt in a long time. Maybe things were going to work out all right. Tom put his arm around me and I felt so safe and protected.

We spent about an hour just lying on the blanket and watching the stars. After a while, though, I began to feel a familiar feeling in the back of my head. I sat up quickly and looked around. Tom sat up, too and asked me what was wrong.

"I don't know. I just have this feeling again. I can't explain it. I haven't felt this since the night of the nuke. I think something is going to happen, but I don't know what."

"Do you want to go back to the house?"

"No, because I am really enjoying being out here with you. I just...I can't explain. I haven't had any nightmares in a long time. There's nothing going on that I know about, but I still have that awful feeling." I laid back down on the blanket. "Let's just stay out here for a little while longer. Maybe it will go away."

Tom agreed, and he laid down next to me. We went back to watching the stars, but I felt very distracted. As I was watching the stars, I noticed tiny black shapes floating through the air. I pointed them out to Tom, and suddenly realized what I was seeing.

"Tom, we need to get back to the house right away."

Tom was still trying to see the little black shapes. "Why, what do you see?"

"Those are paratroopers. I think we are being invaded." Suddenly, we heard the alarm bell ringing back at the house. We grabbed the blanket, tossed the wine bottle and glasses back into the plastic bag, and ran back to the house. When we arrived, there was a flurry of activity on the front porch. Frank was busy giving directions, and people were headed in all directions.

I was out of breath when I reached the porch. "What's going on?" I asked.

Frank answered that he just received a radio message from Mark, who reported paratroopers were landing somewhere between the airport and here. "Mark told us to assemble the militia and to get our kids to safety. He thinks they are headed towards the airport, but we don't want to take any chances. I am sending all of the young kids and non-militia adults to the basement. Mark has extra soldiers on the outer berm, and Chris and Jon are in the OP."

I thanked Frank for the quick report and told him, "We saw the paratroopers jumping. It must have been a high altitude jump because we did not see or even hear any aircraft."

Tom jumped in and suggested we both change out of shorts and sandals, as it looked like it was going to be a long night.

A half an hour later, Tom and I were both back, dressed in our cammies and sturdy boots and well-armed. The two of us headed over to the barracks area to find Mark and see what needed to be done. We found him in the middle of a briefing to his troops. We edged closer so we could listen. Mark nodded to us and continued talking.

"I just got a call from Carter in Riverdale. There are several hundred paratroopers landing somewhere between here and the new base. The community at Whispering Pines has its militia standing ready to repel anyone that attempts to enter the town. In addition, the Ranger instructors and twelve of our soldiers are there to provide added support." He turned to the non-commissioned officer in charge of the Marine squad. "Gunny, I want you to take your squad and find these guys. Make sure they are not coming our way and follow them. I'm sure they are headed to the base, but if it looks like they are coming near us, you need to let us know."

The Gunny saluted and gathered his men. Before they left, he turned back to Mark and asked about the rules of engagement. Mark answered, "Do not fire unless fired on or if you need to protect American citizens. Check in frequently and keep us appraised on what you are seeing." He turned to everyone else. "The same rules of engagement apply to everyone. We won't start anything, but we sure will finish whatever they start."

Mark continued to give direction to his troops, establishing additional surveillance on the outer berm and placing several mortar teams just behind the outer berm. He then instructed us to tell Frank to position the militia around the inner berm. He suggested we make sure everyone had extra ammunition, and that we had people positioned to refill magazines as necessary. He also suggested we make sure everyone had extra water, as it would probably be a long wait. Finally, he told us that if we heard blasts of the air horn, we should be sure everyone was taking cover, as he would only blast the horn if enemy engagement was imminent.

Tom and I hurried back to Frank and relayed all of Mark's directions. The three of us then helped get everyone into position, and made sure each person had water, food, and extra ammunition. We then headed to our battle stations on the front porch and began to wait.

CHAPTER FIFTEEN

General McPherson was meeting with several of his commanders when he received an urgent radio message from the Airport Tower informing him the radar operators were picking up a large number of planes headed towards Riverdale at high altitude. "We can't say for sure that they are coming here, but if they are not headed here, they will still fly directly over us."

"Can you tell what kind of planes, and how far away?" asked the general.

"We think they are C-17s. It looks like there are about ten or eleven of them, and they are about 30 minutes out from here," answered the person in the tower.

"Sound the alarm and send Sammy and Carter over here," he instructed. Less than a minute later, the sirens began to wail. Two minutes later, Sammy, Carter, and Kevin Halvorson came running into the conference area. The general told them what was going on.

"Get this base buttoned down quickly," he instructed. Sammy got on his radio and began issuing instructions to his troops. Carter, meanwhile, turned to the general. "If they really are C-17s, they could be dropping troops to surprise us. Let me get a couple of Ranger companies out there to be ready for them when they land. We've also got some huge spotlights sitting on the short runway. If the tower sees paratroopers, we can have them light them up – that would take them by surprise and help our guys know exactly where they are. Hopefully, we can avoid battle if we can get these guys peacefully. If not, though, they will be easier to overcome if the element of surprise is gone."

The general looked hard at Carter and gave a one-word order: "Go." Carter took off to get his Rangers and special ops troops placed, and Kevin got on the radio to get some airmen to move the spotlights and start the massive generator that powered the lights. Within minutes, the base was swarming with activity as troops took up various battle stations. Calls were made to the Joint Chiefs to let them know what was happening, and the community at Whispering Willows was also notified. In less than ten minutes, the base was as ready as it was going to get. The general got on the radio and let everyone know not to fire until the enemy opened fire.

With about five minutes left until the planes would arrive, there was little left to do but wait. General McPherson listened to the flurry of instructions being issued over the radio. Suddenly, the spotlights on the runway came on. The three men hurried outdoors to see the distant tiny shapes of paratroopers. Suddenly, the shower of soldiers stopped. The tower notified the general that the planes were turning rapidly away.

"Any idea of how many jumpers?" he asked the tower.

"Negative, General, but if there were paratroopers on all the planes, it does not look like all of them jumped. I'm going to guess maybe three or four planes worth."

"Thanks," the general answered. He looked at Sammy. "That would be around three or four hundred if the planes were full. Heck, a company of Rangers ought to be able to take care of that." Sammy smiled, but looked worried. He continued to listen to the traffic on the radio.

Carter raced with his Rangers to the area where he anticipated Homeland troops would land. He warned his troops not to fire first, and to try to take as many as possible captive. As his men faded into the forest, he pulled out a bullhorn.

"Attention Homeland Soldiers. If you throw down your weapons and surrender, you will not be harmed. Your leaders have deserted you. You must have seen all of your planes turn around and run when we put spotlights on all of you. You are surrounded by Rangers and Special Forces troops. We do not want to harm fellow Americans. Your war is over. Throw down your weapons and surrender and you will not be harmed." He waited a few minutes and then repeated the message. Suddenly, through the forest, he saw several of his troops escorting a group of paratroopers. They brought them into a clearing and sat the men down. A few minutes later, another large group of prisoners were marched into the clearing. Carter heard a radio message from one of his teams to the medical tent requesting assistance. Carter interrupted the message to ask who was hurt. The ranger answered, "There are a bunch of these guys here back in the trees that did not know what they were doing and got all tangled up. We've got a number of broken bones and a couple of them that didn't make it."

Carter called back, "we can send some trucks to get the injured when we've rounded everyone up." Carter looked at the rapidly expanding number of prisoners sitting in neat rows and began to wander among them. He noticed that not all were Americans; there were a number of UN troops interspersed among them. For the most part, the captured troops were docile and followed the directions of their captors. There was one group, though, that seemed very defiant, requiring additional troop supervision. Carter walked closer to the group and recognized the ringleader of the group. "Lester Barnes, what are you doing here? I thought you would still be in jail?"

"Homeland let me out of jail, and I am here to kill you and your precious general," Barnes answered with a snarl.

Carter addressed the troops guarding Barnes and his group. "Barnes was one of my Rangers in Afghanistan until he was caught torturing and murdering villagers. He was dishonorably discharged from the Army and sent to jail."

Carter's troops shook their heads and looked at Barnes distastefully. Suddenly, Barnes said, "Now" and the five men with him jumped up and lunged at Carter. The troops guarding them shot each one before they reached Carter. Carter looked down at the bodies in front of him. "Somebody take out the trash when you have time," he said, turning around and walking away.

The group of captive soldiers were ferried back to the college campus adjoining the base. Several classrooms were being used to hold the large group of men. A number of officers were identified among them, and they were segregated from the other prisoners. One at a time, they were brought to one of the small offices next to the classrooms and interrogated. Carter took the highest-ranking prisoner, a full bird colonel, to interrogate.

"Colonel, you know how this works. I need information from you, and I don't want to waste time with all of that name rank and serial number nonsense. A year ago, we would have been working together in the same Army. Let's just dispense with the formalities and get right to the point. What was the purpose of this jump?"

The colonel looked defiant for about thirty seconds, and then must have realized he was caught and did not have much of a chance for escape. "What assurances do I have from you that if I talk, I won't be sent back to the Homeland troops to be killed?"

"I have no intentions of sending anyone back to Homeland, and I have no intentions of harming people who cooperate with me."

The colonel pondered Carters words for a minute or two, then answered. "We were supposed to be backup for a small team of men who were going to kill your general. Once the general was dead, the rest of us were supposed to hold the base to use for Homeland troops."

"Who were the men who were going to kill the general?" asked Carter, suspecting he already knew the answer.

"The six men that were shot in the field. They were a special death squad who carried out specific assassinations for Homeland command."

"Why were there so many troops injured or killed in the drop?"

"Most of us were forced to go, and many of the men, especially the UN troops, had never jumped before. They got a two-minute class once we were on the planes, but that was really not enough. Most of them had to be pushed out of the plane. I'm surprised there were not more injuries."

"Were the UN troops willing to engage with us?"

"No, just the opposite. Most of them were here because they were promised land and gold if they defeated you. They were forced onto the planes at gunpoint."

"Who is calling the shots at Homeland command?"

"It is a cluster of people- and I use the word cluster intentionally. General Bates is the military officer in charge, but there are a couple of politicians who are also giving orders, even though they know nothing about military strategy and tactics. They spend a lot of time arguing about their next move, and then General Bates ignores them and does what he wants. It is almost a free-for-all at times."

"How do you know so much about what is going on at Command?" asked Carter suspiciously.

"Look, I was a staff sergeant working as a radio operator at command headquarters. When this plot was hatched, one of the senators said I looked like a good commander and promoted me to colonel and put me in charge of all these men. I don't know what in the world I am doing here. All I want is to go back to Montana to my wife and kids. I wish I never got involved in this mess."

"Why did you stay with Homeland when so many other members of the military did not?"

"I was stuck. I was one of General Bates' radiomen before and he liked me. I did try to get away, but my escape was foiled when one of the guys got caught. Thankfully, he did not give the rest of us away, but I knew if I tried to leave, Bates is crazy enough to come after me. So, I stayed."

"Tell me about the politicians with Bates. I expect they are all Democrats, right?"

"Actually sir, that is not true. There are a couple of Republican senators who not only agreed with this whole fiasco, but they took part in carrying it out. They called themselves old guard republicans who did not like the current president and didn't agree with the way he was doing things." The 'Colonel' went on to share the names of the politicians who were involved, and Carter could feel himself getting angry.

"What else do these radicals have planned?" Carter asked.

"I don't know. There was no backup plan if this failed – at least not that I know about. I know that they do not have access to the nuclear arsenal – it was a fluke that Bates had the one missile he used on Bragg. I also know they have been in cahoots with China. China set off the EMP in exchange for California. It makes my blood boil that those politicians would just hand over so many Americans to the Chinese." Carter silently agreed with the staff sergeant.

"Okay, Colonel or Sergeant or whatever... I am going to return you to your men, but we will be talking again."

Three hours later, Carter, Sammy and Mac were sitting in Mac's office. Carter had finished reporting the results of his interrogations to the two generals. Mac had taken copious notes to report to the joint chiefs. The men were struggling with what to do with close to three hundred prisoners. The three men were silently thinking, when Sammy had an idea.

"Why don't we decide which ones are UN and which ones are American. We can deport the UN ones back to wherever they came from. Then, maybe we can send the American troops to Leavenworth to stand trial."

Carter nodded in agreement, but then asked, "What about those troops who wanted to leave but were forced?"

Mac answered, "I see where you are going with this, Carter, but let's let the folks at Leavenworth decide that. Besides, it will be easier for your staff sergeant to get home to Montana from Leavenworth than from here."

Carter shook his head and smiled. "You can always see through me, Mac."

Mac grinned and responded, "Yes, that's why I have four stars and you only have one. I'm going to go report all of this to the Joint Chiefs."

CHAPTER SIXTEEN

The night after the paratrooper invasion, Jer, Sue, Jeff, and Bill were on patrol on the north side of the farm. The night had been quiet so far, and the four were about to stop and eat dinner when they heard a faint rustling in the leaves somewhere ahead of them. They proceeded slowly with rifles up and ready. Up ahead was a clearing and soon they could hear a soft murmur of conversation. As they approached the clearing, they saw three men sitting on the ground. Two were eating, and one was writing in a small notebook. They were all in uniform, but it was not the familiar multicam they were used to seeing. In addition, two of the three men had light blue berets, while the third had a light blue helmet. The men looked tired and dirty, as though they had been traveling for a long time. One of the men had his arm in a makeshift sling. Bill quickly stepped through the leaves and shouted, "Put your hands up!" The men looked startled, and then quickly raised their hands. Jer, Sue, and Jeff came through the brush and formed a circle, pointing their rifles at the surprised men. The man who was writing in the notebook looked at Bill and said in heavily accented English,

"Please do not shoot us. We mean you no harm."

"Who are you and what are you doing here?" Bill asked.

"We were with the UN forces, but we left them. What we were being asked to do was wrong, and so the three of us decided to leave. The only reason we signed up with the UN was that we wanted to come to America."

Bill nodded to Jeff. "Jeff, search them and remove any weapons. The rest of you stand fast." Jeff quickly stripped the three men of rifles, knives and handguns. He also put their packs out of reach of the men. Bill spoke quietly into his radio, and then turned back to the three men. "You can put your hands down but keep them where I can see them. You move, and we shoot. Now tell us who you are and where you're from and why you are sneaking around in our woods."

The same man responded. "My name is Gunther Wendt. I was a sergeant in the German army. The man on my left is Jürgen Hambrecht. He was a corporal. The other man is Wilhelm Weber. He, too, was a corporal. Now we are deserters from the UN and we are ...I don't know the English word. *Asylbewerber.*"

Jeff answered, "You are looking for asylum, is that correct?"

"Yes," answered Gunther. "*Sie sprechen Deutsch?*"

Bill quickly jumped in. "English, please. Yes, he does speak German, so be careful what you say to each other. I have called for assistance from our local military unit. They will be here shortly and will want to ask you questions." The men suddenly looked panicked and terrified.

"No, please, just shoot us now. The military will torture us and kill us anyway when they run out of questions. Please, we just want to live in peace. Please do not turn us over to the military authorities." Gunther was shaking, and his face had become very pale. Bill had no doubt that all three men were scared out of their wits.

"I don't know why you would say that. Our troops do not hurt peaceful people. If you give them any reason to think you are not peaceful, that is different, but the troops we work with are good men." Bill shook his head, perplexed at why these men would expect torture and death from American troops.

"When we were with the UN forces, we watched as Americans picked up strangers. They did awful things to get them to talk, and after they gave up all their information, they were shot. Please, we do not want that to happen to us."

"Are you sure they were American soldiers?"

"They were part of your Homeland Security force. They even threatened UN forces that if we did not do what we were told, the same would happen to us."

"The soldiers who are on their way are not part of the Homeland force, and they will not harm you unless you act like the enemy." Just then, Bill heard people approaching through the brush. He indicated to Jer to see who was coming and Jer reported it was Mark, Scooter, and Jimbo. As soon as the prisoners saw the oak leaf on Mark's collar, they stood up at attention and saluted. Mark returned their salute and indicated for them to sit.

"I am Major Schmidt, and I am the commanding officer of this area. Who are you?" Gunther repeated the same story he told Bill, introducing the other two men. "How many others are with you?"

"We are by ourselves. We did not want to stay with those people. They were cruel, and we could not do some of the things they told us to do. They wanted us to take people's food and shoot them if they did not give it to us. That was not a good thing to do." Mark looked intensely at all three men. Each man looked as though he was about to faint under Mark's scrutiny. Finally, Mark relaxed and called Jimbo. "Zip tie their hands and we will take them back to my office for more questioning."

He then turned back to the men. "Your belongings will be returned to you if I find you are telling the truth. Are any of you sick or injured?" Gunther shook his head. "Wilhelm broke his arm when we landed, but other than that, sir, we are tired and hungry, but we are in good health." Each of the men cooperated as their hands were secured, and then the entire group headed back to the RV Mark was using as an office. Jer and Jeff picked up the men's packs and weapons and carried them back.

Mark called me on the radio and had me meet him at his office. He said I should bring my German dictionary if I needed one. That had me very curious. I assumed he needed me to translate something, but he was very cryptic on the radio. When I got to his office, I was very surprised to see three men with their hands zip tied. Mark introduced me to the men as Major Armstrong. I gave him a quick look and he nodded at me. He explained that the men were German soldiers serving with the UN forces, and only one spoke English. He wanted me to be sure the other men understood what was being said, and that they were not trying to communicate with each other in German. I was grateful for my time in Landstuhl and that I tried to keep up with my language skills over the years. Mark explained he would ask the question in English and I would translate if they did not understand.

"Where were you born?"

I repeated in German, "Wo bist Du geboren?"

Jürgen replied "Ich wurde in Bad Lauterberg geboren - in 1995." Mark looked at Wilhelm and he answered "ich auch - 1996." He then looked at Gunther. "Same question." Gunther answered,

"I was born in Bad Sachsa in 1994. Bad Sachsa is only a few kilometers from Bad Lauterberg. We were all friends as children and joined the army together."

"Next question. What were you doing in the forest?"

I repeated, "Was hast du im Wald gemacht?"

Gunther answered, "We explained to the other man. We left our assignments because we could not do the things the Americans were telling us to do. We came here to help, not to hurt people. They were monsters. We made plans to desert when they told us we were parachuting in. None of us every jumped before, but it made sense that we could control our direction by pulling on the strings, and so we intentionally veered away from the other troops. Unfortunately, Wilhelm hit a tree branch on the way down and hurt his arm."

As the conversation went on, it was easy to see the men relaxing under Mark's calm and firm but friendly questioning. Soon Mark had each man's life story, right up until they volunteered for the UN assignment. Their stories were very similar to what was experienced in the United States. When our economy collapsed, the economies all over the world also collapsed. In Germany, there were riots, food shortages, and other violent events just like here. Jürgen's parents had been killed in an accident about a year before the collapse. Wilhelm's father died of a heart attack right after he was born, and his mother and older sister were killed in a home invasion right after the collapse started. Gunther was an orphan who was raised by elderly grandparents. He was told his grandparents were killed when their house was burned down during the winter.

"Why did you volunteer?" he asked.

"We were told that if we volunteered to come here and help America get their traitors under control, when the war was over, they would give us each a piece of land and let us stay here, plus they would pay us in gold. Since we really did not have anything to hold us to Germany, it sounded like a good way to get a fresh start in life."

"If we were to let you settle here, what could we expect from you?"

"We would be loyal to you and to this country. We just want to be able to live in peace, to have an opportunity to maybe someday raise families, to have a place to call home. Germany is not home any more. We have some skills we would be happy to share, and we would do our part to help your recovery efforts."

"And what would you expect from us?"

"We would hope to be allowed to live as free men, but we would not expect anything except a chance to earn our place."

"What can you tell us about what the UN is planning?"

Gunther paused and thought. "I am not sure what they are planning. We were told we were coming here to help protect America from a renegade president and his radical supporters. We were all promised if we wanted to stay we could, and we would be given the land and gold as I already said. But when we got here, we found out the renegades were actually the people who are trying to take over this country. They told us they wanted us to help the citizens, but everything they told us to do was harmful. There are some leaders in the UN forces who agree with the American Homeland troops. Most of the UN soldiers, though, are like us and do not agree."

Mark asked a few more tactical questions about locations of various headquarters and troops. Finally, when he had the information he was looking for, he told the men they would be held under guard until he was able to validate their information.

"I'm not going to keep you as prisoners if what you told me is true. Until then, you will stay in this RV and I will post guards outside. You can relax, clean up, and I will send some dinner over for you. I will also send a doctor over to look at your arm." The three men looked very surprised. Mark continued, "I regret your experience with the thugs in the Homeland forces. They do not represent the American military. We do not shoot people for not giving up food. We don't take people's food. In fact, we work hard to try to take care of the citizens of this country. I'm going to go check out your information, and I will be back."

Mark and I left the men sitting in the living room of the RV. As we stepped out, I noticed four guards outside the RV, two by the main door and two around back by the rear door. Mark saw me looking at the guards.

"I believe these guys, and I think they could possibly be good members of our community if their story checks out. Of course, I'm not about to let them loose until I check out the information they gave us. I'm pretty sure the General will want to talk to them, too. Thanks for your translation services, by the way."

"You are most welcome," I answered. "I was wondering about that. As much time as you spent in Germany, I would think you spoke enough German to interrogate them."

Mark laughed. "I don't want them to know I understand them. I have a microphone in the trailer recording their conversation. That will help me decide what to do with them."

I grinned at his deviousness. "Would you consider letting them live at Whispering Willows?"

Mark grinned back. "That's exactly what I was considering, but it all depends on if their story checks out and if the folks at Whispering Willows agree."

CHAPTER SEVENTEEN

Two days after the landing, General McPherson called all of his command officers to the big conference room. Mark, Tom, and I were also invited to the meeting. I was pretty nervous, as I knew whatever it was the general was going to tell us must be pretty serious to include Tom and me. General McPherson entered the room, followed by Sammy and Carter. Once everyone had taken their seats, General McPherson stood up in front of the room.

"Thank you all for being here this morning. Things have been pretty crazy here for the last couple of days, but I have news to share with all of you. It seems a lot has been going on while we've just been sitting around here." There were a few nervous chuckles, and the general continued. "First of all, the UN is withdrawing all troops. It seems they got wind of their troops being forced onto the planes at gunpoint without proper jump training, and they are angry. Our navy is overseeing the complete evacuation of the UN from the east coast. That includes all of the staff of the UN in New York that did not comply with the President's demands last year that they leave. When the Homeland planes landed back in Washington, most of them still full of troops, General Bates met the planes at the airport. He was screaming at the men and calling them cowards. One of the UN troops shot him and was then shot by the military policemen with Bates. With Bates dead, the troops in Virginia were in limbo. The politicians kept issuing orders to the troops that just did not make any sense. Half the Homeland troops holding the line in Virginia just walked away. Some joined the Patriot lines, and some just walked off. Our Rangers and the militias in that area were able to take advantage of the confusion among the Homeland troops and attacked. They basically wiped them out. We now have Rangers in Washington and moving up the coast cleaning up the mess. The traitors holding the President were overcome, and our President is now free. There is still sporadic fighting going on in pockets around the east coast, but the command and control elements of Homeland have been captured or eliminated."

All of us stared at the general in shock. A Captain at the table found his voice first. "You mean, it's over?"

Mac nodded, and everyone began cheering. The general let us all cheer for a few minutes, but then reined everyone in. "There will still be a lot of clean-up to do, but I think all of the major fighting is over. We were told to interview the American troops we are holding. If they seem to still believe in Homeland's message, we are to send them on to Leavenworth. If they are able to convince us they are done with the fighting, we can let them go. I did tell the Joint Chiefs that if we let them go, we will ferry them to a point very distant from here so they don't have much desire or ability to come back.

"California will be the next area to tackle, but it probably won't be as easy to wrap up. The Chinese are heavily embedded in California right now. The President is sending the Fourth Infantry

Division our of Fort Carson, Colorado and the 101st Infantry Division out of Fort Campbell, Kentucky for a joint operation to rid California of the Chinese troops. Between the Iron Horse and the Screaming Eagles, I suspect they will make quick work of the problem. At least our troops from here should not be involved with that. We'll have enough to do to make this area safe from people who want to take advantage of the situation.

"There will be a lot of work to do to restore this nation to what the founders intended it to be. Government will need to be rebuilt and infrastructure will need to be repaired. The EMP caused far too many deaths across the country. Citizens will need help rebuilding homes and lives. Above all, there are also a lot of divisions to be healed. The President says that has to be one of the biggest priorities." People were nodding agreement with all the general was saying.

"Meanwhile, America is declaring its Second Independence Day! I will address the troops this afternoon. Mark, please go announce this in your community. Denise and Tom, let your folks know, too. The President plans to address the country by radio in the next few days, as soon as someone can get the radio station broadcasting again."

Sammy raised his hand to ask a question. "General, you never did tell us why General Bates hated you so much!" The general began laughing.

"It started out when I married his girlfriend – well, his ex-girlfriend, I should say." Everyone laughed, and the general added,

"After that, he competed with everything I did, and got angry if things went my way. He never did get over Sheila choosing to marry me, and even blamed me when she died a couple of years ago from cancer. Yes, he was a real fruitcake, and the world is way better off now that he is dead."

When we arrived back at the farm, Tom and I called everyone together. We even called in the troops manning the berm. Once everyone was assembled on the front lawn, Tom and I stood on the porch to share the news. There was a lot of cheering and more than a few of us burst into tears of happiness that the war was over, at least for us. Finally, people settled down and we could continue. We explained that there would be a lot of work to be done and things wouldn't change all that much for a while from what we had all been experiencing. Finally, amidst all of the happy chatter, Tom let out a really loud whistle to get everyone's attention.

"There is still one matter that needs to be addressed." He turned to me and said, "We've all lived through the end of the world as we know it, right?" Everyone nodded and a few people called out their agreement.

"We lived through an almost civil war, right?" Again, there were nods and yells.

"We lived through the collapse of the economy, right?" Suddenly Tom looked at me very intensely.

"I know that we all lived through some horrible things together, and we don't know what the future might bring us. I do know one thing, though. Denise, I don't want to go through the future without you by my side." The crowd got very quiet as he got down on one knee and took my hand. "Denise, will you please marry me – soon before anything else happens?"

The crowd erupted into cheers and catcalls, but I didn't notice. I could only see the love in Tom's eyes as I answered firmly, "Yes."

EPILOG

It has been five years now since the economy collapsed. Life on the farm is not much different now than it was then. Tom and I were married by Father Dan in our little church. It was a beautiful ceremony and I could not believe how many people came to celebrate with us. General McPherson played the role of Father of the Bride and walked me down the aisle. My sons were in the front row, and both were beaming with happiness. It was a wonderful day that I will never forget.

The population of the farm has changed a little over the last five years. Chris and Stacy had three more children, a little girl and twin boys. Jose and Maria also had another baby. Jeff and Sue decided two years ago to get married, and now they are the parents of a sweet little boy. The Culler family, our neighbors that came to stay with us, moved back to their home when the war was over. It took a lot of work, but with help from the guys on the farm, they were able to restore their home and make it livable again. Kiara recovered from her injury, and she and Lionel were married shortly after Tom and me. In addition to their adopted kids, Amaya and Freddy, they now have two more kids. Anaya and Freddy love their new brother and sister and spoil them rotten.

We've also had a couple of losses in our farm family. Simon McIntyre passed away in his sleep a few months ago. Sarah took his death rather hard, but the children gave her a reason to keep living. He is buried up on the hill next to Red and my grandparents. We also lost Tory Chen a couple of years ago when a flu swept through the farm. Thankfully, all of the others who were sick recovered, but the loss of a sweet little girl was devastating.

The war in California dragged on for months after we declared victory on the East Coast. Eventually, though, our military prevailed and the last of the Chinese troops were removed. California was devastated by the economic collapse and the occupation. Hollywood was just another neighborhood and all of the California millionaires became ordinary people, just like the rest of us. There was a short attempt for the southern part of California to secede, but that effort died quickly when they realized there would be no economic support for them as either a new state or as an independent country.

The President pared down the government significantly. Layers and layers of bureaucracy were peeled back, and only the bare minimum government remained. The governor of North Carolina survived and did the same thing in the state. Two years ago, we finally held elections, and the President was re-elected by a huge margin. There is no longer a democrat or republican party. Both had gotten derailed a long time ago and neither accurately represented the desires of the people. For now, people all run for office as independents, standing not on party lines, but on their own beliefs and philosophies. I am sure that down the road new parties will emerge, but for now, this seems to be working. Our nation is again a Constitutional Republic.

The community of Whispering Willows has grown and is thriving. There are now several hundred families living there. The school is again full of happy children, the strip mall is reopened for small businesses, and Top, who retired from the military, was elected as the community's first mayor. All of the Ranger instructors still live in the community, and they now run a new Ranger training area several miles north of the community in the forest.

The base at Riverdale continued to grow as well. In addition to the airport and the college, the base is also now using some of the space from the destroyed downtown area. A new community has sprung up just outside the base and has become the new Riverdale. General McPherson is still the commander of the base, but he is talking of retiring soon.

Infrastructure across the country is growing slowly. Many areas still do not have power, but more and more power plants are slowly getting back on line. With our solar, we never really were troubled by the loss of the grid, and neither was Whispering Willows. The big wells that were dug when we first started working in Whispering Willows are still working, and almost all of the homes there now have running water. The base built a hydroelectric plant on the river, and that is powering the base and also the small Riverdale community.

It has been a crazy few years, but we survived. I believe our survival was due to several things. First, being prepared helped us initially to make it through that first difficult winter. The second thing that helped us was the genuine love and affection we all had for each other. People question how so many people can all live together through difficult times without fighting with each other. I believe it is because we all had so much respect for each other that disagreements were handled quickly and amicably. The third thing that helped us was our faith. It did not matter what religion each person was; what mattered was that we all shared a common set of beliefs and values, and we tried to live by them. I think the last thing was our belief that we lived in the greatest country on the face of the planet. We wanted our nation to survive, and in order for that to happen, we had to do whatever we could to help our fellow citizens. Our military played a huge role in our success as a community, and we are so happy that the base with so many of our friends has remained in Riverdale.

Life is good now. It is a lot simpler than it was six years ago before all of this mess happened. In some ways, it is much better. We still do not have a national currency, so all of our "shopping" is done through bartering. That works. We no longer have welfare or other "entitlement" programs. Instead, we help each other. There are no more nursing homes; our elderly are cared for at home. We don't have a hospital yet, but Lionel and James are working with Top to build one between Whispering Willows and the farm. Reflecting back on all that has happened, it is amazing what good people can do when they try to do the right things. We tried, and we succeeded.

Yes, life is good now.

APPENDIX

-

Cast of Characters

People living at Langston Farms

Denise Langston Armstrong: 52, RN educator, owner of Langston Farm, widow

Christopher Robert Armstrong, ("Chris"), 26, Denise's son, older twin

Stacy Mabry Armstrong, 24, Chris' wife

John Henry Armstrong, newborn son of Stacy and Chris

Jonathan Michael Armstrong, ("Jon"), 26, Denise's son, younger twin

Gabriella DeVeaux Armstrong, ("Gabby"), 25, Jon's wife

Amelia Danielle Armstrong, Jon and Gabby's newborn daughter

Tom VanZant, Denise's contractor and friend, 54

Marcie Evans, 49, RN, worked on Medical Surgical Unit

Frank Evans, 51, deputy sheriff, former Marine, Marcie's husband

Grace Evans, 22, Marcie and Frank's daughter, student

Mandy Evans, 4, Grace's daughter

Lisa Manzini, 34, RN, worked in operating room

Charles (Chuck) Manzini, 41, worked in gun store, now responsible for the farm's armory

Jeremiah ("Jer") Manzini, 16, Lisa and Chuck's son

Nathaniel (Nate) Manzini, 14, Lisa and Chuck's younger son

Maureen Flinn, 50, RN, worked on labor and delivery unit

Clark Flinn, 50, veterinarian, Maureen's husband

Sarah Flinn, 15, youngest daughter of Maureen and Clark,

Phoebe Flinn, 16, Maureen and Clark's middle daughter

Zoe Flinn, 18, Maureen and Clark's oldest daughter

Samantha Rivers Werther, 42, RN, worked on Medical Surgical unit

James Werther, MD, 44, surgeon, Samantha's husband

Janet Livingstone, 42, worked on Medical Surgical unit, in charge of food preparation

Martin Livingstone, ("Marty"), 43, carpenter, Janet's husband

Samuel Livingstone, 14, Janet and Marty's oldest son

Michael Livingstone, 12, Janet and Marty's youngest son

Patricia Schmidt, ("Patty"), 51, RN, worked on Medical Surgical unit

William Schmidt, ("Bill"), 53, police officer, ex-Army, Patricia's husband

Daniel Ellington, ("Father Dan"), 58, Catholic priest, expert at all things radio.

Judy McCleary, 52, Tom's sister, married to Timothy McCleary

Timothy McCleary, 58, carpenter/electrician/mechanic

Jose Contreras, 38, carpenter

Maria Contreras, 32, Jose's wife

Savannah Alvessa Contreras, ("Chica"), newborn daughter of Maria and Jose

Lionel Wilkes, 43, physician and best friend of James Werther, significant other to Kiara

Amy Chen, 28, RN, worked for Lionel, significant other to Jimbo

Tonya Chen, 6, Amy's daughter

Tory Chen, 4, Amy's daughter

Tyler Chen, 2, Amy's son

Lynn Jessup, 37, Dr. Wilke's office manager, significant other to Top

Marvin Reddick, ("Red"), 23, Lynn's brother, carpenter

Jeffrey Solomon, 17

Susan Lewis, 16

Elaina Lewis, 13

Mariah Peters, 13

Thomas Peters, 11

Billy Peters, 7

Drake Goins, 12

Anaya Goins, 6

Freddy Goins, 4

Simon and Sarah McIntyre

Military

CPT Mark Schmidt, 31, Patty and Bill's son

1LT William Roland, ("Billy"), 29

2LT Alicia Roland, ("Allie"), 27, Billy's wife

1SGT Marcus Harper, ("Top"), 46, significant other to Lynn

SGT James ("Jimbo") Wyatt, 29, significant other to Amy

CPL Paul Wilson, ("Scooter"), 26, significant other to Grace

1LT Kiara Diamond, 34 significant other to Lionel

COL Carter Murphy, 50, commander of local military troops

General Wayne ("Mac") McPherson, 58

COL Samuel ("Sammy") Iverson, 56

COL Kevin Halvorson, 52

2LT Peter Braxton, 24

Anita Braxton, 23, Peter's wife

Private Nicky Cooper, 21

ABOUT THE AUTHOR

Diana E. Anderson

Diana was born and raised in New York. She majored in foreign languages in college and after graduation, joined the army as an interrogator/ translator with language specialties of Chinese Mandarin and German. After completing military service, she went back to college and obtained her degree as a Registered Nurse. Almost four decades later, Diana has held a number of staff and leadership positions in nursing and is currently an Infection Preventionist for a rural health care system. She also served as a nurse in both the North Carolina and Texas State Guard. She went back to college several times throughout the course of her nursing career, eventually earning a doctorate degree in health administration. She lives with her husband and two very spoiled cats names Boris and Natasha. In addition to writing, Diana enjoys reading, genealogy, and shooting.

THANK YOU FOR READING!

If you enjoyed this book, we would appreciate your customer review on your book seller's website or on Goodreads.

Also, we would like for you to know that you can find more great books like this one at www.CreativeTexts.com

www.ingramcontent.com/pod-product-compliance
Lightning Source LLC
Chambersburg PA
CBHW030641110726
47901CB00002B/535